Chelsea spent the past ten years rebelling against Zane's control. When her parents died, he became her guardian, controlling her trust fund and the company they shared. But hating the control he exerted on her did nothing to stop her from wanting him.

When she refuses to obey his summons for a weekend meeting, he cuts off her money, leaving her in a strange city with no way to pay her hotel bill. Forced to accept his help and join him at his country house, she soon discovers his intention is not strictly business. When she experiences his potent masculine domination she finds the reality of being with Zane far exceeds her fantasies... leaving her wanting more.

But can she surrender to this forbidden love and be mastered by her guardian?

Other Books by Opal Carew

St. Martin's Griffin
My Best Friend's Stepfather
Stepbrother, Mine
Hard Ride
Riding Steele
His To Claim
His To Possess
His To Command
Illicit
Insatiable
Secret Weapon
Total Abandon
Pleasure Bound
Bliss
Forbidden Heat
Secret Ties
Six
Blush
Swing
Twin Fantasies

Single Title Novels
Taken By Storm
Debt of Honor
Crystal Genie
Slaves of Love

Ready To Ride Series
#1: Hot Ride
#2: Wild Ride
#3: Riding Steele
#4: Hard Ride

The Office Slave Series
#1: The Office Slave
#2: The Boss
#3: On Her Knees

Three Series
#1: Three
#2: Three Men and a Bride
#3: Three Secrets

Red Hot Fantasies Series
#1: The Male Stripper
#2: The Stranger
#3: The Office Slave

Anthologies and Box Sets
Red Hot Fantasies
Three Happy Endings
Northern Heat
Turn Up The Heat

Mastered By My Guardian

Opal Carew

Mastered By My Guardian

Discover more books by Opal Carew at her website
www.OpalCarew.com

Book Design by **Mark's Ebook Formatting**
Email: **mark@MarksEbookFormatting.com**

First edition: July 2015
www.OpalCarew.com

Mastered By My Guardian

Chelsea walked across the lobby with her suitcase and carry-on in tow, headed to the huge lineup of people waiting to check out. There'd been some big conference at the hotel while she'd been here and it seemed like all of them were checking out at the same time and none of them knew about express checkout.

She sighed, thinking of the note she'd found slipped under her door this morning, telling her there was a problem with her credit card and asking her to stop by reception. She stepped behind a tall woman with a wide-brimmed hat and her smaller companion who were chatting in a language Chelsea didn't recognize.

Her cell phone chimed and she pulled it from her purse.

"So how's New York?" asked Sandy, her office manager and close friend.

"It's fine. It's New York."

The women ahead of her in line moved forward so Chelsea grabbed the handles of her suitcase and carry-on in one hand and awkwardly dragged them forward to keep up.

"You don't sound very excited. I'd *love* to visit New York."

“Yeah, well, I come every year at this time to meet with the lawyers and sign the endless papers they collect up for me.”

Just another way Zane kept control of her. Insisting she had to come to the city to meet with the lawyers in person rather than just receiving the documents in the mail. But he was in charge of the corporation that she reluctantly shared with him. At least she’d gotten him to agree that he no longer be present while she met with them. His cool, dominating presence just unnerved her.

“So when are you coming back?” Sandy asked.

Chelsea frowned. “You know I’m coming back today.”

“Yeah, but I thought maybe you might change your mind. You really aren’t going to stay for the weekend? Aren’t you worried he’ll get mad?”

Chelsea shrugged. “Why should I care if he gets mad?”

“He is your stepfather. And he controls your trust fund.”

She pursed her lips. “He is not my stepfather.”

In fact, Zane was her guardian. He was the son of her father’s business partner and when both their parents had died in a plane crash when she was sixteen, Zane being ten years older than her, had become her guardian. It was efficient, since fifty percent of the shares were bequeathed to her, but he controlled those shares through a trust, so even now, she had very little say in the company. But she hated being under his thumb and had decided a couple of years ago that she'd build her own company and let him have at it with No Limits, the high tech conglomerate that led the market in memory chip technology.

"Whatever. Do you really want to defy him?

She frowned. "Screw him. I'm not going to drop everything and come running every time he decides he wants a meeting. He never listens to me with respect to NLI anyway."

"Okay, well I'll see you when you get back. Maybe we can catch a movie together."

Chelsea smiled. "Yeah, I'd like that."

Sandy had been her friend ever since she'd moved to San Diego two years ago. They had a lot of laughs together.

After she hung up the phone, she glanced at the line-up. It was moving pretty fast, but it looked like another ten minutes at least. She decided to check her email.

Finally, she was at the front of the line waiting for the next available reception clerk. A man finished paying and moved away, then the young man behind the counter signaled for her to step forward. She rolled her suitcases to the desk.

She opened her purse and pulled out the notice she'd received under her door this morning, then placed it on the counter.

"I was informed there's some problem with my credit card," she said.

The clerk glanced at it, then at her. "Yes, Ms. Barrett. Just a moment." He picked up a phone and called someone, then turned his attention to her again. "If you would just step to the side for a moment. Someone will be over in a second to talk to you."

She pulled her bags to the side, a little annoyed that he waved another person over, leaving her standing here.

"Ms. Barrett?"

She glanced around to see a tall man in a crisp suit standing beside her.

"I'm Mr. Diegler, Assistant Manager. If you'll come with me we'll get this whole thing straightened out as soon as possible."

"Good. I'm sure it's just some sort of mistake." The card was nowhere near the limit and the expiry date was two years from now.

She followed him across the lobby and down a short hallway to an office. It had a nice view of the colorful potted plants at the entryway of the hotel.

She sat down in the chair facing his desk as he sat behind it.

"As I said, there must be some kind of mistake, because—"

"There's no mistake. We called the bank and they confirmed that the card has been deactivated."

Her stomach clenched. "But that's impossible."

This was the only card she had and she had no other way to pay for the hotel bill. The urge to pick up the phone and call Zane zipped through her brain, but she knew that was just a panic reaction. She would not turn to *him* for help.

Surely there was some other way.

"But I… don't understand," she said in a shaky voice.

He held up his hand. "Please, don' worry. The bank staff told me there was a note on the account giving a phone number of someone at your company that could straighten things out."

"Oh," was all she could manage.

Mr. Diegler handed her a slip of paper with a phone number written on it. She didn't recognize the number.

She pulled out her cell phone and dialed. It only rang once before someone on the other end picked up.

"Hello, Chelsea."

At his deep, smooth as silk baritone voice, anxiety coiled through her.

It was Zane.

Through gritted teeth as the realization of what had happened sank through her, she said, "God damn. Did you have a stop put on my credit card?"

* * *

Chelsea marched out the front door to the limousine she'd watched pull up in front of the hotel from Mr. Diegler's office window.

Zane's limousine.

It annoyed her no end that all it had taken was a few words from Zane to Mr. Diegler to clear up the whole issue. Mr. Diegler had hung up the phone saying the bill had been taken care of and she was free to go.

She should have known better than to keep using the credit card attached to her trust, but the limit was so much larger than she could get on her own, either personally or through her still growing business. If she hadn't been able to get Bill to invest, as well as finding that angel investor, she never would have been able to start the business at all.

Except that Zane had told her he would loan her the money to get started, but she'd known that was a ploy to keep her under his thumb. She wanted nothing to do with him or his money.

This company was hers and had nothing to do with Zane Chase.

The driver opened the back door of the limo. She knew Zane was in the car the moment the door opened even though she didn't glance inside. His presence was palpable. She slid inside, taking a deep breath to calm her nerves.

"It's nice to see you, Chelsea."

"Yeah? I can't say I feel the same way."

She glared at him, but almost faltered at the sight of his incredible eyes, a blue so clear and deep she'd always been mesmerized by them. He smiled and the curve of his full lips, contrasting his strong, square jaw, was just so incredibly masculine, yet alluring, her heart raced. It was always like this. His intensely masculine presence threw her totally off kilter and his extreme good looks set her heart pounding.

But she hated him. Hated how he tried to control her.

"Why did you cancel my card?"

"How else was I going to ensure you spend the weekend with me?"

She raised an eyebrow. "You don't really think I'd spend the weekend with you after that stunt, do you?"

"Then why did you get in the car?"

"I assumed you'd give me a ride to the airport. After all this, I'm running late." She glanced at her watch. "I need to be there in thirty minutes."

"I'm not driving you to the airport."

"Then let me out and I'll get a cab."

"Really? And how do you intend to pay for it?"

"Cash," she lied.

He laughed. "I doubt it. You never carry more than twenty dollars."

It was true, She relied on her debit and credit cards for most of her needs. And she had a sinking feeling he'd put a hold on her account, too. He certainly had the power to do it.

"So you're basically kidnapping me?"

"I think that overstating it, but…" He shrugged. "You really left me no choice. I repeatedly invited you and you refused. The same thing happened last year. But if you like, I can drop you at the corner and you can contact your business partner and have him wire you some money."

But they both knew she wouldn't do that. She wouldn't want to look weak in front of Bill, either for being controlled by Zane or needing to rely on Bill for money.

She scowled, wishing she had been smart enough to get a separate credit card that was not connected to her trust a long time ago.

Though a little voice inside her insisted that with Zane's knowledge of trusts and all things financial, he probably had a way of controlling her that went beyond her reliance on the trust.

She crossed her arms, seething as she turned her head to stare out the window at the traffic around them, trying to ignore his dominating presence beside her. It was going to be a long drive to the country house in Connecticut, and she had no intention of making small talk with him.

She sank into the supple leather seat, resting her head back facing away from him, then closed her eyes. She was tired and the feel of the moving car soothed her. As annoyed as she was, after a while she felt herself dozing off.

"Chelsea, we're here," Zane said softly.

Her eyelids popped open and she sat up, fighting the comforting feel of his voice curling through her.

He smiled. "You always did have trouble sleeping the day before travel."

She frowned, hating that he knew her so well.

She glanced at the large mansion with the lovely garden out front and the stone path leading to the impressive entrance. Double doors with beveled glass that glinted in the sunlight, two large potted plants on either side filled with tall green plants and colorful flowers.

The driver opened the car door and she stepped out. The lilacs were in bloom and she breathed in the sweet scent, unable to stop a smile from curling her lips. She'd always loved lilacs. The unbidden memory of Zane planting those bushes after their parents died flashed through her brain. Her father wanted an orderly garden with neatly groomed, very traditional plants. For some reason, he didn't consider lilacs to be among them.

But Zane had known she liked lilacs and put them in that very first summer. That action had seemed so at odds with everything else she remembered about that time.

As the driver retrieved her bags from the trunk, Zane took her arm to lead her along the path, but she tugged her arm free and walked on her own. He didn't push it and just walked along beside her.

When they reached those impressive doors, she waited while Zane unlocked them. As soon as she stepped inside, her breath caught as potent emotions bubbled through her. This was where she had lived with her parents. Memories of her mother's smiling face and how she always used to greet Chelsea at the door after school made her heart ache. She missed her mother so much. Especially being held by her and feeling the love of being so truly and lovingly cared for.

She glanced around. When she'd first come here as a child, she'd been enamored of the huge chandelier hanging in the entrance because of its myriad of glittering crystals. And she'd always wanted to use the heavy oak banister of the large, curved staircase as a slide, but her father would never allow it.

Her father had had a lot of rules. She thought things would change when Zane became her guardian and moved in, but he'd had his own rules.

The driver entered the house with her bags.

"Take them up to the first bedroom on the left," Zane instructed.

"No," Chelsea said. She did not want to stay in her childhood room. "I'd rather one of the guest rooms."

Aside from the desire to keep old memories at bay, she also didn't like the idea of being right next to his bedroom. But Zane directed the driver to take her bags to the bedroom across the hall. Since his room was the width of the wing, that bedroom shared a wall with his, too. But she wasn't in the mood to fight about it.

She followed the driver upstairs.

"Come down by seven o'clock," Zane instructed. "I have a meal prepared."

She just nodded, too tired to argue.

She got settled in her room. It had been redecorated since she'd last been here and it was exquisite in jewel tones and cherry furniture. Her cell phone trilled, indicating a text message, which reminded her she'd meant to text Bill as soon as she got here.

She sat down on the chaise longue and grabbed her cell phone from her purse, then pulled up the text from Bill.

Where are you? I thought you were returning today?

It turns out I'm staying the weekend, she tapped in. *I was just going to text you.*

You weren't on the flight. I was worried.

He'd come to meet her? She hadn't expected that. Now she felt badly that she hadn't let him know sooner. Bill seemed to be looking out for her more than usual lately and she'd been getting the impression that maybe he wanted to evolve their relationship beyond just a business partnership to something romantic. Bill was an attractive man and they had a lot in common. And he was very respectful of her opinions, something she hadn't been used to before meeting him, but the idea of getting involved with him… She wasn't sure. Which was crazy because everything indicated that they'd be perfect together.

Sorry, I just got to the house. I'll be in Connecticut until Monday.

I can't believe you decided to stay after all. You were adamant you wouldn't.

Yeah, things changed. I'll tell you about it when I get back. Have a good weekend.

It was actually Thursday, so for her it would be a long weekend.

She put away her phone and pulled out her tablet, then read some of the emails she'd had on hold. After she finished that, she noticed her watery eyes and runny nose were back. She always got this way when she traveled and the allergy medicine she'd taken earlier had worn off, so she retrieved another from her purse and took it.

Damn, tension thrummed through her at being stuck here under Zane's control, but she had no intention of obediently trotting downstairs at seven o'clock as instructed. She knew there would be a confrontation, but that was still an hour away. She decided to take a nice hot bath to reduce her stress. Soaking in the big tub was nice, but when she got out and pulled on her silk robe, her stomach was still wound in knots. She settled on the chaise again and began to read a book on her tablet.

At seven fifteen, a loud knock sounded at the door.

"Chelsea, I told you dinner was at seven."

Had he really believed she would simply obey after what he'd done? Of course, she knew he did. He was that arrogant.

"I'm not hungry."

"You are, but clearly you intend to be stubborn. I insist, however."

She glared at the door. "You can insist all you want. I'm not coming down."

Then her breath caught as she heard a key in the lock and the door opened.

In all the time they'd lived together, he'd never breached a locked door. He'd always allowed her that level of control.

Clearly, things had changed.

His stern gaze caught on her, then drifted down her body and over her legs, searing her.

God, it had never been… he'd never looked at her like that.

She had felt a strong attraction to him, she couldn't deny that, but he had always been cool. Detached.

But at this moment, the heat in his gaze could make her go up in flames.

She pulled her robe tighter around her as she stood up. She wished it was longer and wanted to tug the hem down to cover more of her thighs.

It was unmistakable. The heat in his eyes was pure, unadulterated lust.

And she felt herself reacting to it. Her insides pulsing with need. Old memories of dreams she'd had when she was eighteen where she'd sneak into his room in the middle of the night and climb into his bed, then convince him to take her body in an intimate dance of passion. Images of his big arms around her… his big cock sliding into her…. claiming her completely…sent her totally off balance.

"I invited you here because I wanted to spend time with you. If you won't come downstairs, then I'll spend time with you here."

Oh, God, no. Wearing only her small robe, totally naked underneath… with his masculine presence dominating the room… she felt far too vulnerable.

She stared at him, knowing her eyes must be wide but unable to hide her discomfiture. She bit her lip and his hard gaze softened.

"Chelsea, I just want to have dinner with you and spend the evening together. It's no big deal."

She drew in a deep breath and nodded, her throat too tight to manage uttering actual words.

"Good. Now get dressed and meet me downstairs in ten minutes."

"Yes, sir." The words just slipped from her mouth.

When he gazed at her, something flickered in his eyes, but she couldn't read the emotion. Maybe he thought she was being sarcastic. Whatever it was, he nodded and left the room. As soon as the door closed, she sighed in relief.

* * *

Zane glanced up as Chelsea descended the stairs. The sight of her took his breath away. She was as beautiful as always. Tall and slim in her tailored dress, but rounded in all the right places. Her chestnut hair, pinned up in a tight coif, was brushed to a high gloss. In fact, all of her was polished, from her designer outfit, to her immaculate manicure. A sharp contrast from the way he'd seen her ten minutes ago.

He couldn't get that image out of his mind. She'd looked all soft and feminine in her short sexy robe, her long hair cascading past her shoulders in gleaming waves. Her bare legs, and the deep, alluring V of skin visible where her robe wrapped around her had been unsettling. He'd wanted to walk up to her and pull that robe open. To feast his eyes on the sight of her naked body beneath.

As much as he wanted her… and from the heat in her gaze, he was sure she wanted him, too… he'd resisted.

But he didn't know how long he could hold back.

When he'd returned from the UK right after their parents had died, he'd been blown away by how beautiful she was at sixteen. When he moved in to be her guardian, he'd quickly realized that his growing desire for her would become a problem. He'd tried to convince himself that she was just too young, that at twenty-six he shouldn't have these feelings for a sixteen year old, but nothing could convince him that he didn't want her. So he'd had to pull back and keep a cool demeanor.

She had been so sweet and lively when she was a child, following him around and always asking questions in her delightful way. Gazing at him as if he'd been the most important person in the world to her. He'd hated seeing that light in her eyes dim, then die out completely. But he didn't know what else he could have done.

Now, however, they were both adults and he longed to have her. Not just to alleviate the almost crippling physical hunger he felt for her, but because he wanted her in his life. Every part of it.

But he knew convincing her would be a challenge beyond measure.

Especially with what was brewing with her company.

Chelsea walked to the dining room and sat down at the table. He had the dinner already set out. He filled her wine glass then sat across from her.

She ate in silence, not giving an inch, but he didn't really blame her. He had trapped her and she didn't respond well to that, but he had to shake her out of her stubbornness.

He filled her glass again, then offered dessert, but she declined.

"Let's sit in the living room and talk."

"Do I have a choice?"

He smiled. “Yes. We could talk in your room.”

She frowned and picked up her glass, then walked to the living room and sat in one of the armchairs by the fireplace. He carried the bottle of wine with them and sat on the couch.

“How’s your business doing?” he asked.

“Fine. A few financial issues, but I’m sure you know that.”

He kept tabs on her business and he knew it bothered her, but he wasn’t going to stop. She was a savvy business woman, but she was a little naïve about some things, and definitely too trusting of that partner of hers.

“Chelsea, I keep informed because I want to look out for you. I care about what happens to you.”

“And you don’t think I can manage a business all on my own.” She raised an eyebrow. “Are you going to offer to lend me money?”

“You wouldn’t take it if I did.”

“Because it’s insulting. Like you’re just waiting for me to fail.”

“You’re being too sensitive. I don’t expect you to fail.”

Her eyebrow shot up. “So you think Quiet Thunder will thrive?”

He compressed his lips. “I think you have some problems to overcome. And you know I have concerns about your business partner.

Her fingers tightened around the armrests of the chair. “Bill was the reason I could get this business started in the first place.”

“What about your angel investor?”

She picked up her wine glass and took a sip. “He’s just a distant presence, putting money into a company he doesn’t care about in the hopes it will take off and earn him a lot of money. Bill is an on-going presence. Helping make the day-to-day decisions,” She stared at him defiantly. “Bill believes in me.”

“Chels, I never said I didn’t believe in you.”

“No, but you show it in the way you try to control everything I do.”

He settled back in his chair. “For the past two years, I have left you alone and let you start this business of yours, while I run No Limits on my own.”

Her eyes flashed. “First, I don’t give a damn about No Limits. You never let me make a decision that matters anyway. And you didn’t *let me* start my business. I didn’t use your money.”

She had used money she’d saved from her allowance from the trust, though, but he wouldn’t mention that. And he certainly wouldn’t mention the angel investor again.

“And I don’t exactly call trapping me here for the weekend leaving me alone,” she continued.

"Since you are here, why don't we put all this aside and just enjoy the weekend?"

Her lips formed a thin line and he knew she would stubbornly refuse to give an inch.

"You know, when you were young you used to look up to me. I remember the first time we went with our parents for their yearly business retreat, you followed me around like a puppy."

"I was seven." She leaned forward and picked up the wine bottle, then filled her glass.

He smiled, remembering the bright-eyed, delightful child she'd been. "Yes, but you did it every year, until I went to the UK for college."

* * *

Chelsea frowned. She remembered. She had adored him.

He'd been a teenager, and had never seemed to mind that she tagged behind him the whole weekend. He'd almost enjoyed it, even though she realized later that he must have been instructed by his father to keep her occupied. Still, she'd always looked up to Zane and had been thrilled at his attention. He'd been this adult who had cared about her having fun. Not like her father.

She had missed Zane when he'd gone to college and so far away. When their parents died, he'd returned to Connecticut and become her guardian. Their first meeting after being apart so many years had been overshadowed by grief. After the funeral, he'd moved into her parents' house but instead of the friendly, caring teenager she'd remembered, he'd become a cool, aloof adult.

She had been looking forward to presenting him with her ideas for the company they now shared, but to her surprise, he had ignored them, telling her she was too young and inexperienced to have any real say in the running of the company. It's not like she didn't realize that at sixteen, she didn't have the experience he had, but he could have listened. He could have tried to work with her.

She'd quickly come to realize that Zane was just as controlling as her father had been.

"Well, I'm not a child now. I'm all grown up."

"Yes, you are."

Her gaze darted to his at the innuendo in his silky baritone voice. The heat in his cobalt blue eyes took her breath away.

"I've had a long day. I think it's time I turned in," she said.

She placed her empty wine glass on the table and stood up. But the world seemed to sway a little and when she took a step, she was unsteady. She moved around the coffee table and focused on walking straight, but bumped into the side of the one of the armchairs.

Zane was on his feet and by her side instantly.

"What's wrong, Chels?"

Her back stiffened. "Nothing. I'm fine."

But her hazy brain combined with his close masculine presence made her stumble slightly. His arm swept around her and drew her close to his warm body as he walked with her.

"I'm fine," she grated.

"You took allergy medication today didn't you? I should have realized that the wine would be a bad idea."

God, he was right.

"You know," he said, "there's nothing wrong with leaning on someone when you need help."

She gave up her resistance and melted into him. His arm held her securely to his body as they walked, but when they reached the stairs, he swept her up in his arms and carried her.

The world whizzed past her as she clung to his neck. Despite her dizziness, she was intensely aware of his muscular arms around her. Supporting her. Of the heat building inside her.

This was insane. She wasn't going to… *He* wasn't going to…

They reached the end of the hall. His bedroom in front of them, hers to the right.

Carefully, he set her on her feet, his arm around her waist to steady her.

"Thanks," she murmured, feeling more than a little vulnerable at the weakness she'd shown.

She turned to her door and reached for the knob.

"This isn't how I'd hoped this weekend would start," he said.

Her cheeks heated. "Having to carry me to bed tipsy?"

He chuckled. It was a sound she hadn't heard in a long time and she realized she'd missed it.

"I mean I didn't want it to start with you angry. I had hoped we could have a serious talk."

She gazed up at him. "About what?"

* * *

Zane knew this was stupid. He should not be bringing this up when they were standing outside her bedroom door, her woozy from a combination of medicine and wine.

"About a change in our relationship. I became your guardian when you were sixteen, but now we're both adults. You have your independence. There's no reason we couldn't let go of those roles and…"

"And what?" she asked when words failed him.

As she stared at him with her wide brown eyes, his gut clenched. She really had no idea what he was suggesting. Fuck!

"Never mind. We can discuss it tomorrow."

She nodded, then turned and opened her door.

"Do you need any help…?"

Her gaze darted to his and she shook her head rapidly. "No, I'll be fine, thanks." Then she shut the door behind her.

* * *

Chelsea leaned back against the door, her heart pounding.

Oh, God oh God oh God. He couldn't have meant what she thought he meant. What a crazy little part of her wanted him to mean.

She walked to her suitcase and retrieved her satin pajamas. She shed her clothes and pulled on the pants, then the top and buttoned it up. She pulled back the covers and knew as soon as her head hit the pillow, that she'd fall asleep right away.

She turned off the light and lay down, but found herself staring at the dark ceiling, the memory of Zane's arm around her, his solid body supporting her…haunted her.

Her eyelids fell closed and she let herself relax as she gave herself over to fantasies of Zane lying close to her, his lips trailing along her neck. His hand cupping her breast. Gliding down her stomach.

She murmured softly as his fingers stroked between her legs, sending heat pulsing through her. His fingers pushing inside her.

Blackness surrounded her as she faded into sleep.

In the shadowy world of her dreams, she opened her eyes and knew she had to seek out what she wanted.

Zane.

She drew back the covers and walked across the dark room. A moment later, she stood in front of his bedroom door and opened it quietly, then slipped inside. Moonlight streamed in the window and she could see him stretched out across the large bed dominating the center of the room. He was asleep, his breathing even.

She walked to the bed and lifted the covers, then slid in beside him. She snuggled close to him, reveling in the comfort of his masculine presence.

* * *

Zane woke with a start, realizing there was a warm body beside him. He glanced at the sweet face resting on the pillow beside his and his eyes widened.

Chelsea had climbed into bed with him. Her arm was around his waist and her cheek rested against his biceps.

His heart pounded with the desire to feel her lips on his. To glide his arms around her and pull her against him, her soft, round breasts crushed against his chest, while he ravaged her mouth.

His groin tightened and he knew the moment he felt her body against his like that, he'd be rock hard and far too tempted to slide into her warm depths and claim her. Even the *thought* of her soft body surrounding him made his cock swell, filling him with a sweltering ache.

He sucked in a deep, slow breath. Why was she here?

She murmured in her sleep and shifted. Her arm brushed against his rock-hard cock and he sucked in a breath. His gaze dropped to her face, but her eyes were still closed and her breathing remained even.

She was asleep.

Sound asleep.

Then he realized…she'd been sleep walking. A smile spread across his face.

She'd been sleep walking and she'd come to him. Climbed into his bed.

Gently he tucked his hand under her neck then slid his arms under her, then drew her close. She murmured softly again and rolled closer still, her head now on his shoulder.

As painful as it was to lie there with her so close while his body ached to make love to her, he lay in the darkness happily, knowing that tomorrow, the world would be a very different place.

* * *

Chelsea opened her eyes to the close-up view of a strong masculine jaw, heavily shadowed with morning stubble. She seemed to be wrapped around the owner of that jaw, her arm snuggly around his waist and her leg curled around his thigh. His hard, muscular thigh.

God, how had she wound up in Zane's bed?

Staving off the panic, she decided to slowly pull away without waking him, then she'd slink out before he knew—

The arm she was lying on tightened around her shoulders.

"Are you awake?" she whispered.

"As a matter of fact, I am."

Damn. She'd hoped his arm tightening around her was just a reflex and she could still escape.

She tried to roll away but his arm was like a steel band holding her in place. Then he rolled toward her, causing all kinds of wild sensations to flicker through her.

Now they were facing each other on the pillow and her heart stuttered.

Oh, God, so many times she'd dreamed of this, but now faced with the reality… Knowing the tensions between them…

Then the memory of last night, when he'd mentioned something about their roles changing…

"I don't understand," she stammered. "I don't know how I wound up… here."

God, she was in his bed. And it was *his* bed, not hers, with the forest green sheets and the navy and green patterned duvet. It was a huge, king-sized bed. Big enough for his huge, king-sized body. A tall, masculine muscle-bound body.

"You climbed in here in the middle of the night." The light dancing in his eyes made her wonder what else she'd done in the middle of the night.

"We didn't…" Her throat closed up and she sucked in a breath. "I mean… nothing happened did it?"

He arched an eyebrow. "You mean you don't remember?"

Blood rushed to her cheeks and her eyes grew wide.

"Oh, God. No. We didn't." Her heart pounded in her chest.

His clear blue eyes grew serious.

"Don't worry. Nothing happened. But..."—he stroked a finger lightly across her cheek, sending her insides fluttering—"would it really be so bad if it had?"

Relief rushed through her, but his blue eyes held her mesmerized.

"I... uh... It's just that..." Oh, God, she didn't know where to go with this.

Then suddenly his mouth was on hers. His firm, full lips coaxing. He drew her closer and the feel of his body the length of hers, his tongue nudging at her lips, sent her pulse skyrocketing. She opened and he glided inside. She melted against his solid body as their tongues entwined, his mouth moving on hers in a passionate play of power where he was totally in control.

And she was loving it.

Then she felt his cock swelling against her belly and shock rocked her to her very soul. She flattened her hand on his chest and pressed against him.

He cupped her head, seducing her mouth a moment longer, then his face eased away. Their gazes locked, his questioning, then he sighed and loosened his arm around her. She scooted back, putting well needed inches between them. At least, for her sanity's sake.

She drew in deep breaths, trying to calm herself.

"Last night," he said, "I told you that I want to talk about a change in our relationship."

"And this is what you meant?" She hadn't intended her voice to have that shrill edge.

"We're both adults now and clearly you're as attracted to me as I am to you."

"Because I climbed in your bed?" She shook her head. "No, that was just me sleep walking."

She hadn't done it in years, but he knew she'd had the problem. He'd been the one who'd taken her to the doctor about it.

"And I don't believe you would sleep walk right into my bed unless that's where you wanted to be."

She rolled away and hopped from the bed then scurried from his room, fleeing him and the disturbing desires his kiss had aroused.

* * *

Chelsea showered and dressed, plagued by the disturbing feelings at waking up in Zane's arms. And the way she'd reacted to his kiss.

It had been… her body quivered… intense and…oh, God she wanted to run right back into his arms now.

She brushed her long, dark hair until is shone. This was crazy. Zane talking about a change in their relationship. As if they could just switch to being…She pulled the brush through her hair again, staring at herself in the mirror…He wanted to be lovers. Her breathing grew shallow. He couldn't really…she couldn't let that happen.

Could she?

She sucked in a deep breath and headed for the bedroom door. As she walked down the stairs, she smelled coffee. She walked into the kitchen and saw Zane standing at the counter, a steaming mug of coffee in his hand.

"Good morning." He moved to the stove and cracked open an egg into a waiting frying pan. "Sit down. I'll have your breakfast in a minute."

She watched as he opened the oven and took out a pan of sausages he'd been keeping warm, then arranged them on a plate.

He was making her breakfast, which was sweet and made her feel cared for, but she couldn't let that affect the decision she'd made.

"I want to leave," she said firmly. "Today."

He used a spatula to scoop up her eggs and place them on the plate. "And I want you to stay."

"You can't just keep me here."

"I'm not stopping you from leaving." He smiled. "I'm just not helping you do it."

And given the fact she had no cash or working credit cards, and the house was a good distance from town, she'd have a hard time getting back to San Diego without his help.

"What if I call the police?"

"And what? Have me arrested for not driving you to the airport and lending you money for an airline ticket?"

Her fists clenched at her side, frustration shooting through her.

His expression softened. "Chelsea, is it really so bad staying here for the weekend and just spending some time with me?"

He set the plate of eggs and sausage in front of her. She stared at it, her stomach rumbling, but she didn't pick up her fork.

He sighed. "Okay, well I have to go out and run an errand. I'll be back in about an hour."

She said nothing as he left the room, but then her hunger got the better of her and she started to eat. She heard him go out the door to the garage and then the sound of the automatic door opener first opening the garage door, then closing it after he'd pulled out.

When she finished her breakfast and coffee, she cleaned up the dishes, then sat down to read. It was quiet in the house and the air outside was still. If she hadn't felt trapped, she might have enjoyed the solitude and the chance to relax. The business had kept her pretty busy, especially with the research team hard at work on a new product for their line of fast charging batteries.

That's what had made her company succeed. Innovative battery technology that allowed a cell phone to be fully charged in less than thirty minutes. It had been an idea she'd pursued when she'd been doing her Master's thesis. Her partner, Bill had been another grad student at the time and had seen the value of the idea and had suggested they partner. They'd attracted an angel investor to help them get started and after only a year, they'd gone public.

Now they had stockholders and a board and all the things that drove her crazy. But they'd also been able to build the business and pursue other ideas, like a battery that could charge from ambient energy, thus requiring no need to plug in. It would allow cell phone owners to keep their phone fully charged as long as they were within twenty feet of a wall socket.

Bill was really excited about it and had been hinting that once they finished this product that they should sell the company, making a huge payback on their investment. That's not what she wanted to do, though. This company was everything to her. It was her baby. It allowed her to be innovative. It allowed her to shine.

Being president of Quiet Thunder made her feel like an intelligent, capable woman. Not like the inept, inexperienced person she felt around Zane.

At a rumbling in the distance, she glanced to the window. It had been gray all day, but now ominous dark clouds filled the sky. A flicker of light made her jump.

Lightning.

She hated lightning. And thunder.

A deep, rumbling sound rolled across the sky, then a flash of lightning filled the room. Her stomach clenched.

She'd been terrified of storms when she was younger. She used to go into the basement where the windows were small and she could barely hear the thunder. She grabbed her tablet and headed for the door leading to the basement stairs. She crept down, sighing in relief when she saw that Zane had upgraded the rec room with cheerful colors and lights bright enough so that it didn't feel gloomy. She sighed as she sank onto the couch.

She read a little, but the basement was not her favorite place to be alone, so she soon became restless. She glanced around at the redecorating Zane had done. There was a hallway off the rec room and she stood up and walked down the hall. There was a bathroom that hadn't been here before, then a door at the end of the short hallway. She walked toward it, wondering what was behind the door. Probably just a storage room, but he didn't really need more storage with a large area with shelves behind a door on the other side of the rec room.

Maybe it was a home theater. Or a room with a pool table. But some instinct told her it was neither of those things. She reached for the doorknob, fully expecting that it would be locked.

The doorknob turned.

Of course. Why would Zane keep it locked? He lived alone.

She pushed the door open and peered inside. She found a light switch on the wall beside the door and flicked it. Lights turned on, but not a bright overhead light. Instead, mood lighting that cast a shadowy light on what she could only describe as a dungeon.

She stepped inside, the door closing behind her, and gazed around at the gray stone walls. There was a big leather chair and couch in deep burgundy leather and rough-hewn, wooden furniture in the room—a tall armoire and various other benches and padded wooden furniture she wasn't sure of.

Then the glint of steel on the wall caught her eye. There were sturdy steel rings protruding from the wall, with thick metal cuffs dangling from chains.

God, what was this place?

She walked to the chains and touched one of the cold, hard cuffs. They were positioned just right to chain a person to the wall.

It looked like Zane was into some pretty kinky stuff.

As that unsettling notion crept through her brain, she thought she heard something and glanced around. She sucked in a breath, realizing how eerie it was in this dimly lit room in the far reaches of the basement. She heard another sound, and swung round to face the door, just as it burst open. Zane stormed in, his face a storm cloud of anger.

She sucked in a breath of relief,

"Chelsea, what the hell… I didn't know where you were."

"You knew I couldn't be far," she retorted. "You haven't really given me a choice to leave." She raised an eyebrow. "Or did you think I'd decided to walk to town?"

"I wouldn't put it past you," he said as he approached, like a panther stalking its prey. "And with the downpour outside… and the lightning…"

He knew she didn't like lightning. That she used to hide away in her room. He didn't know that she used to sometimes come into the basement, so she couldn't see or hear the thunder and lightning.

But back then there'd been nothing like this room down here.

"I wanted to get away from the lightning." She didn't know why she revealed that to him.

He stepped closer. “I’m sorry.” Concern etched his face. “I didn’t mean to leave you alone in a storm. I know how much they bother you.”

He hadn’t said that she was afraid of them. He hadn’t diminished her by making her sound like a fearful child.

“It’s okay. I can take care of myself.”

His gaze searched hers, the depth of concern in his cobalt blue eyes unsettling.

“I kept thinking of you outside, wandering through the woods, with the lightning flashing and the boom of the thunder…I didn’t like to think of you alone and dealing with that.”

“I would be perfectly capable of dealing with the situation.”

He ran his hand from her elbow to her wrist. “You’re trembling.”

She stepped back to put distance between them, but he followed. The stone cold wall pressed against her back.

“It’s cold down here. I think we should go upstairs,” she said.

But he didn’t budge, his big, masculine body trapping her against the wall.

“I think we should talk about our relationship.”

She tried to step sideways so she could dodge around him, but he grasped her arm.

"Are you going to keep running away from this, Chelsea?" he demanded.

"I'm not running. I just want to go upstairs," she insisted.

"The storm's still pretty bad."

She hesitated at the thought of flickering fire flashing across the sky, followed by the horrendous boom of the thunder, making her feel as if the sky would crash down on her at any moment.

But she drew back her shoulders ready to protest more vehemently. Then a flash of light past the open door startled her, followed by deep, rolling thunder echoing through the room. Her chest constricted. It was close, leaving her unsettled. In fact, Zane's presence helped ground her.

She glanced up at him as she realized he was lifting her hand. Her cheeks flushed when she realized she'd actually linked fingers with his. She was holding his hand.

Before she realized what was happening, he snapped one of the cuffs hanging from the wall around her wrist. Her eyes widened. He grasped her other hand and snapped the other band around that wrist.

"What are you doing?" She hated the tremble in her voice.

"I'm making sure we have this conversation."

She stared at him as he turned and walked to the door, but he didn't leave as she'd suddenly feared he would. He closed the door. Keeping the storm out.

She pulled on the bands restraining her wrists. The chains clanked. The metal wrist cuffs had looked ominous hanging on the wall, but they were lined with thick, soft fabric so didn't hurt her wrists.

He walked toward her, an ominous figure in the shadowy room.

"You're really going to keep me chained up while we talk?"

"Yes," he said simply.

His presence filled the room and as he got closer, she found it hard to breathe.

"Zane, stop kidding around and let me go."

"Chelsea, I'm dead serious. We are having this conversation."

He stood only a breath away. His closeness sent shimmering awareness through her.

"And I like you like this." His lips turned up, but his striking blue eyes held no hint of humor.

Oh, God, he had this room—this… dungeon—in the basement. That meant…well, he must like to…

Damn, images of him having kinky sex with beautiful women sent her totally off kilter.

Did he want to take her against this wall? Drive his big, solid cock into her?

Her knees went weak.

"Okay, you want to talk." Maybe if she cooperated, he'd let her go. "I'm sorry I haven't taken more of an interest in No Limits. If you want me to, I can—"

"That's not at all what I want to talk about." He eased a breath closer, making her heart race. He stroked a hair from her face, sending tremors through her. "I want to talk about this attraction between us. I want to talk about why you climbed into my bed last night—"

"You already know that was just—"

"And I want to talk about where it's going."

"It's not going anywhere. I'm *not* attracted to you."

"Really? I don't believe you."

She frowned. "I don't care if you don't believe me. It's true."

He cupped her face, his hands warm on her cheeks, then his lips found hers. His tongue pressed against her lips until she opened, then drove inside. The feel of him exploring her moist depths made her dizzy with need and when he released her mouth, she sucked in a breath, her gaze locked on his intense blue eyes.

"I've wanted you forever," he murmured, "and I can see that same need in your eyes."

She shook her head in protest.

Annoyance flashed in his eyes. "You can lie to me, but for God's sake, don't lie to yourself."

His arm glided around her and he dragged her tight to him, then took her lips again. The quivering pleasure of his kiss held her mesmerized… until she felt his other hand between them, slowly moving down the front of her blouse. Oh, God, he was releasing the buttons.

She turned her head, jarring her lips free. "No, Zane."

He eased back and gazed down at her, then drew her blouse open, revealing her simple floral lace bra beneath.

"It's so pretty and feminine. It suits you."

His praise didn't stop her cheeks from flushing hotly at him gazing at her intimate garment.

"Zane, this has gone too far."

"On the contrary. It hasn't gone anywhere near far enough." He eased her blouse past her shoulders, letting it drape from her arms. Then his gaze fell to her breasts and with what could only be described as awe, he ran his hands over her them, caressing lightly, then cupping them in the warmth of his hands.

His touch was so gentle and loving.

He leaned forward and pressed his lips to her breast, then sucked through the thin fabric. To her total shock, she arched against him.

Trembling with need she leaned back against the cold wall, willing herself to protest. But his touch felt so good.

His hand glided down her stomach and she tensed as it slipped inside her jeans.

"No, Zane."

But too late. His fingers had already slipped between her legs and found the dampness there. He unfastened her jeans and pushed them down to her knees. Still crouched in front of her, he stared at her skimpy, floral panties. His fingers glided lightly over the fabric which was damp from her excitement.

He stood up, now sporting a smug, masculine expression.

He pulled something from his pocket and then she felt metal against her skin near her shoulder, then the bra strap released. She glanced at his hand to see a pocketknife, which he was using to cut the second strap.

"My bra," she protested.

"I'll buy you another one."

His hand glided behind her and he unhooked it. The bra fell open. He pushed it out of the way and it dropped to the ground.

He stared at her naked breasts, heat blazing in his eyes. Then he swooped down and his mouth found her swollen nub and she gasped at the intensity of feeling herself drawn into his hot, moist mouth.

He suckled and she arched, wanting more.

The sound of a zipper, then the feel of his hot shaft falling against her stomach, jarred her from the haze of pleasure. It was thick and hard, and felt like molten iron as it glided over the crotch of her panties, then he pulled aside the fabric.

"Zane, no, you can't do this," she says weakly.

His determined gaze, melting with need, locked on hers. The tip of his cock brushed against her naked flesh.

"Tell me you don't want this." The hard flesh brushed against her again. So thick and solid.

She ached for it inside her.

"I don't… ohhh…" she moaned as he brushed against her again. "I…"

He pressed his cheek to her temple, his hot breath rippling across her neck, sending tingles through her.

"I want you. I've wanted you for a very long time." His cockhead swiped over her moist folds again, sending heat fluttering through her. "And clearly you want me, too."

"We can't," she protested, desperate to maintain some level of sanity.

"We can do anything we want. So if you want me to stop, tell me right now that you don't want me."

He stared and she struggled to find it inside herself. To tell him the lie.

But she had never been able to lie to him.

And she had wanted him for such a long time. She used to lie awake at night, wishing he'd come into her room and take her. She'd wanted him to take her virginity and show her how to be a woman. And she'd hated herself for it. Wondering what was wrong with her. But now, as she stared into his demanding blue eyes, she couldn't deny it.

His lips turned up in a smile and his hard flesh stroked over her soft folds again. His lips captured hers, pressing her head hard against the stone wall as her insides ignited with flames at the feel of his erection brushing her sensitive flesh. Then he pressed, pushing his hot, hard cock forward. Inside her. Just a little at a time.

She shook his lips free and sucked in a breath, but he captured her mouth again and drove his tongue deep as his cock pushed further into her. Stretching her.

Oh, God, it was so big. So devastatingly hard and imposing.

And it felt so good pushing inside her.

She moaned into his mouth and he released her lips, then watched her as he pushed deeper. Eyes wide, she was mesmerized, staring into his hard-as-iron gaze. But there was something more there. Something almost… soft.

Desire for her?

Lust made more sense. Just the need to control and subdue her, and why not sexually, since he was right, there had always been a strong attraction between them, even though they had both always known it was too taboo to pursue.

He pushed deeper, his body now crushing her to the wall. Now he was inside her. Completely immersed in her. What was the point of fighting it now?

She just stared at him, both of them breathing hard.

Then he drew back, and drove forward again. Sparks flared inside her. As he drew back, her breath caught at the feel of the ridge of his cockhead dragging along her sensitive flesh, then she gasped as he drove deep again.

He began to pick up the pace, his erection gliding within her in powerful strokes, filling her, then gliding away, until he almost pulled free entirely, then driving deep again. His enormous cock filled her so full she thought she'd burst.

"I'm going to make you come," he murmured against her ear, stirring the fine hairs along the side of her neck. "And when I do, you're going to call out my name."

He pulled back and drove into her again. Pleasure swept through her as his hard flesh filled her. The feel of his body tight against her stole her breath away. And the feel of him invading her body sent her hormones spiraling.

He drove deep again. She sucked in air as the intensity of the sensations built, swelling into a wave of joyous desire.

She wanted more. Needed more.

His lips nuzzled her neck, sending more tingles dancing down her spine, and the feel of it was so tender… so intimate… she lost her hold on the here and now. She arched against him and moaned, pleasure bubbling through her, buoying her higher and higher. Ripping her from reality and flinging her to rippling heights of frantic pleasure. Her wrists fought against the restraints as she tried to reach for him. To cling to him.

He thrust into her like a jackhammer… filling her so full… so fast and hard. She moaned, longing to hold him close, then her thoughts shattered and she trembled as bliss shuddered through her. She gasped.

"Oh, God, Zane. Yessss!"

Then she wailed long and hard, sure her screams must be deafening him, but he kept pummeling her body with his long, hard…oh so thick and delicious.… cock.

Then he groaned, pinning her to the wall, and exploded inside her. The feel of his hot seed filling her jolted her pleasure higher.

Finally, she collapsed against the wall, the stone cold and hard against her naked skin.

She felt the restraints around her wrists release and he scooped her up and carried her toward the stairs, then to the main floor. She clung to his neck, her head resting against his shoulder as he headed to the curved staircase leading to the second floor. Bright light flashed through the large bay windows and he held her a little closer, but the lightning didn't bother her, nor did the roll of thunder following on its heels as he bounded up the stairs. The steady beat of his heart against her ear… the protective feel of his arms around her… made her feel safe.

They reached his bedroom and he opened his door. A door that she'd never opened before last night, but had always wanted to. She'd always wanted to know what it was like in his bedroom. His inner sanctum.

She'd seen it this morning, but only briefly as she'd fled his bed. Now it was too dark to see anything more than the huge bed in the middle of the room, the thick posts at each corner of the wooden frame glowing slightly in the illumination from the hallway.

He pulled back the covers and lay her down, then slid in behind her. His arm glided around her waist, and he pulled her close. Lightning flashed and he drew her tighter to his hard, muscular body.

She relaxed against him, feeling safe in his embrace, despite the storm raging outside. His lips brushed against her temple and she sighed, not wanting to think about what had just happened between them. And how she had wanted it just as much as he had.

And what it might mean.

* * *

Chelsea awoke to the feel of warm lips caressing her forehead. She murmured her approval as she snuggled closer to the solid body in front of her. As her eyelids fluttered open, the lips found hers in a gentle kiss. It was dark and she couldn't see, but she knew it was Zane. She was in his room. In his *bed.*

His hand covered her breast, enveloping it in warmth and she ached for him. She wanted… Oh, God, she needed to feel his hands on her. Stroking. Caressing. She curled her hand over his shoulders and slid one hand along the breadth, then up his muscular neck to his jaw. He sighed then his tongue gently glided into her mouth. Her tongue met his and they undulated together.

His thumb found her nipple and stroked. She arched against him. He released her lips and eased her onto her back, then his mouth found her nub. The hot, moist feel of him on her took her breath away.

"Oh, God. Yes," she moaned as he licked and fondled the hard bead of her nipple with his tongue.

Then he suckled and she gasped at the pleasure spiking through her. His hand stroked down her hip, then glided between her legs. She arched her hips upward. As his fingertips trailed along her inner thigh, the sensitive flesh pebbling into goose bumps, she yearned for him to touch her in her most intimate place. Then to glide inside her.

He brushed over the crotch of her panties, then slid under the fabric to her soft folds. She could feel the slickness as his fingertips teased her flesh. She opened her legs, inviting him inside. Oh, God, wanting him inside so badly she thought she'd die.

But he just glided over the surface and back to her hip.

His teeth grated over her hard nipple and she arched again, pushing it deeper into his mouth. He closed around her and sucked. She gasped at the wild sensations bursting inside her.

She surged her hips upward, wanting him to satisfy her craving. She bumped against his rock-hard erection. Her hand glided down his chest and she found it. Hot and thick. Her fingertips brushed the length of his shaft and then she wrapped her hand around it and stroked. She smiled at his guttural groan of approval.

She could see him now in the dim glow of the moonlight, her eyes adjusting to the darkness.

He leaned on his elbow, his gaze locked on her, as she stroked his hard cock. He seemed to rumble as he shifted forward and she felt her panties glide away then his leg nudging at her thighs. She parted them as he prowled between her legs, his big body hovering over hers, his gaze still pinning her to the pillow. He ran his hand down her stomach and brushed her intimate flesh, his fingertips exploring the dampness of her folds. Then instead of slipping away again, this time his finger dipped inside… just a touch… and she moaned.

He pressed his hard cockhead to her opening, and she waited, breath held, wanting his invasion more than anything she'd wanted in her entire life.

His lips brushed her temple. "Say yes."

She hesitated, just wanting to feel him deep inside her.

He drew back, his glittering gaze trapping hers once again.

"Say it."

"Yes," she murmured, the word trailing in an almost hiss.

Then he thrust forward, his thick, hard cock invading her again. She cried out in joy, squeezing him as he surged deep inside her. His body pinned her to the bed and she clung to him, just like she'd wanted to when he'd made love to her against the stone wall in the dungeon.

"God, I want you so badly," he said, clinging to her, holding her tight to his broad, muscular chest.

Then he drew back and pulsed forward. His cock filled her impossibly deep, its breadth stretching her wider than she'd ever been stretched by another man. She tossed her head back against the pillow.

His lips found her neck and he nuzzled. "Tell me you want me, too." As he said it, he drew back, his cock slipping to the edge, ready to pull all the way free of her body.

Desperate not to have him leave her, she scratched at his back, trying to pull him in again.

"Yes, I want you, too. Please."

He smiled, then drove forward, filling her with a swirl of desperate need and wild delight. As he drew back again, she clutched him with her passage, trying to prevent his escape. Then he thrust forward again.

"Oh, God. It feels so good." Her voice trembled, as if she was close to tears, and maybe she was. The sensations were so intense.

So good.

She stroked his naked ass. God his butt was so hard and compact. He pushed deep into her again and the muscles in that fine ass tensed under her hands.

She squeezed, loving the feel of the hard flesh in her grip. He groaned and thrust harder.

"Oh, God," she cried.

He was so deep she could barely stand it. But she wanted him deeper still. She pulled his ass hard against her. He thrust deeper, then grabbed her knees and hooked them over his shoulders. When he thrust again, she gasped as he went impossibly deeper still.

"Oh, yes. I'm…"

His thrust stole her breath. She gripped his shoulders.

"I'm so close," she continued, panting against his ear.

"Me, too, princess." Then he thrust deep again.

As his big cock invaded her body again and again, she began to moan. He was so thick… so hard. Driving her pleasure higher and higher.

"Ohhhh," she moaned as he thrust again, her tender passage stretched. She could feel him deep inside her.

"I'm going to come, baby. Are you with me?" he murmured against her ear.

She nodded, dizziness throwing her senses off balance, pleasure swelling inside her like a hurricane. Then she squeezed around him and the pleasure burst within her, propelling her over the edge, into a long, shattering freefall. She clung to him, as he continued pounding into her body, and wailed her release.

He groaned and thrust deep, his pelvis pinning her to the bed, and shuddered against her. Her mind twirled, her body melted. She dissolved into a vibrating mass of pure pleasure. Humming. Spinning. Expanding into an ecstatic vortex.

Then fading. She held him tight as she slowly returned to earth. Becoming conscious of the sound of their heavy breathing filling her ears. Of the feel of his heart pounding against hers.

She rested her head against him and sighed.

That was sensational.

And she didn't want to think beyond that.

His arms tightened around her and his lips nuzzled her temple.

As she started to doze, she felt him roll to his side, then she felt herself pulled closer against him, her head resting against his chest, the steady beat of his heart soothing her. She sighed and faded off to sleep again.

* * *

Zane knew the moment Chelsea woke up. He'd been holding her close, her soft body snug against his. He was as close to heaven as it was possible to be.

She was his.

But as soon as she woke up, he could feel her body tense. She blinked her eyes at the bright sunlight streaming into the room—her long, dark hair, mussed around her face, glistening like a halo. Then she gazed up at him. Her brown eyes, flecked with gold, held a look of uncertainty that tore at his heart.

"Good morning," he said.

Her cheeks flushed. "Hi."

Silence fell between them, then she started to roll away, but he curled his arm around her and drew her back, preventing her escape.

"Going somewhere?" he asked, gathering her close to him.

"I should shower and… um… I could make breakfast."

He smiled. "That's very nice, but I'm not letting you go just yet."

She gazed at him with wide eyes. For so long she had kept a distance between them, defying him at every turn, but now she looked vulnerable and confused.

"I think we should talk," he said.

"Over breakfast?" she asked hopefully.

"No, right here." He drew her tight to his body, her naked breasts pressing against his chest. So soft and… God, his cock ached as it swelled.

He kissed her, his lips moving on hers passionately, and though she resisted at first, soon she melted into the kiss. When he released her, her breathing was erratic and her expression dazed.

"What happened between us last night is real," he said. "I wanted it. You wanted it. I want us both to be clear on that. Understood?"

"You're talking to me like I'm a child."

He smiled and his hand cupped her soft breast. The tight bud of her nipple spiked into his palm.

"Sweetheart, you're a full grown woman. A fact I totally appreciate. Now tell me about your reservations so we can work this out."

"I don't know… when our parents died and you became my guardian." She pursed her lips. "You took care of me."

"And I want to keep on taking care of you. But not as your guardian."

He kissed her neck, then nuzzled under her jaw. Satisfaction filled him as he heard her breathing accelerate. But she planted her hands on his shoulders and pressed him back.

Her expression filled with concern. "You know I don't like being controlled, but that's what you do."

He stroked a wisp of hair from her face, gazing at her, his heart filled with love.

"Chelsea, I know you feel that's what I'm doing, but I'm just being protective of you and looking out for your happiness. I've only ever meant the best for you. It's not because I have an inherent need to keep you under my thumb."

“This is just such a shock. When you first moved in here…to take care of me… why were you so cold?”

His heart ached as he realized how alone that must have made her feel.

He shook his head. “You were sixteen. I was ten years older and I wanted you so bad I could barely stand it. I had to keep a distance between us.”

* * *

Chelsea shivered as Zane brushed her cheek with his fingertips. The deep sadness in his intense blue eyes made her heart ache.

“I’m sorry if it caused you pain,” he said. “I never intended that. I just…” He shook his head. “I didn’t know what else to do.”

Oh God, she wanted to pull him into her arms. To melt against him and tell him she would be his forever.

But could they really make it work? Could their relationship change from what it had been to… them being lovers?

Did she want it to change?

“Tell me what you’re thinking,” he insisted.

“I… just don’t know what it will be like.”

His broad smile filled her with light.

"It will be intense and fulfilling." He nuzzled her neck sending tremors through her. His hand glided up her stomach. "Exciting." His hand cupped her breast and her nipple peaked. "Intoxicating."

Oh, God, she believed him. It would be all those things… and more.

Her arms slid around his neck and she pulled him in for a kiss. As soon as his lips found hers, her resistance slipped away, and she lost herself in the kiss, knowing she would be his for as long as he wanted her.

* * *

Chelsea couldn't stop smiling. This long weekend that she had dreaded had turned into something quite extraordinary. Her dreams of being with Zane had become a reality and that reality far exceeded the fantasy. Aside from the time in the dungeon, he had been tender and loving, and the adoration in his eyes made her feel incredibly special.

But the taste of dominant male from that first time left her wanting more. He naturally took charge and the thought of submitting to him in the bedroom was…appealing. But it also unnerved her. She'd spent the past ten years rebelling against his control. The idea of surrendering to it now confused her.

Zane had some business calls he had to make, so she poured herself a soda and walked into the living room, gazing out at the colorful flowers in the front garden. She grabbed her laptop and sat down at the desk in the corner of the living room to check her email. As the computer started up, she noticed a blue envelope on the desktop. Zane's name and address were handwritten. She lifted the envelope, which had been opened and saw a card underneath.

A birthday card.

Her gaze shot to the calendar and she realized…oh, God, today was Zane's birthday.

Her breath caught as she realized that's why Zane had invited her here this weekend. So she'd be with him on his birthday. And she had refused to come. Last year, too.

When she was younger, he had always made a point of celebrating her birthday, making it special with gifts and a special dinner. As she'd gotten older and rebelled against his controlling nature, she'd refused the celebrations, telling him she didn't want them to continue celebrating birthdays, then been a little annoyed when every year he sent her a beautiful bouquet of flowers. She had just wanted to be free of his rule and would have preferred to sever all ties to him.

It hadn't occurred to her that since she was the closest he had left to family, that maybe the celebrations were important to him.

Oh, God, when had she become so self-absorbed that she'd totally shut out his needs. He had looked after her for so many years, ensured she got a good education, that she lacked for nothing…and she couldn't even make him feel special on his birthday.

She stood up and closed her laptop. This year would be different. She would make it up to him.

She didn't have a gift, but she was sure she knew something he would like.

* * *

Zane walked from the den to the living room expecting to find Chelsea waiting for him. He couldn't believe his dream had become a reality and he'd finally made her his. Of course, keeping her would be its own challenge. But he would do everything he could to make her want to be with him.

He glanced around the living room but Chelsea was not there. Maybe she was in the kitchen. He smiled. Or waiting for him in the bedroom, but he knew that was just wishful thinking. He walked into the kitchen but there was no sign of her there. He returned to the living room, thinking maybe he'd been right about the bedroom after all. He walked to the staircase and noticed a burst of tightly curled red ribbons hanging from the banister. The coils were tied together by a single ribbon that trailed to the floor and disappeared down the hall.

He followed the ribbon to the door leading to the basement. He turned the knob and peered down the stairway. The light was on and he could see the ribbon continue down the steps. He followed, a smile curling his lips. What was she up to?

When he reached the dungeon door, he opened it and his breath caught. There kneeling on the floor was Chelsea, her head bent downward. His heart rate accelerated at the sight of her in a black leather harness he recognized from the collection he stored in the dungeon cupboard. The straps surrounded her breasts without covering them and encircled her torso. She wore a leather thong that revealed her shapely ass.

The red ribbon he'd been following led straight to her, and was tied to the leather collar around her neck. A flood of tight ribbon coils fell from the collar as if she were a gift.

"Chelsea?"

"Master Zane, I wish you a happy birthday and intend to do whatever I can to please you on your special day."

His smile broadened as his heart raced. "You're saying that you're my birthday present?"

He'd been sure she'd forgotten. And maybe she had, but she was certainly making up for it in a spectacular fashion.

"Yes, Master. I surrender to you completely."

Joy bubbled through him and he laughed. The thought of her bending to his will, especially given her rebellious nature toward him, sent his cock twitching.

"Stand up and come here. I want to look at you."

She stood up and walked toward him. The heels she wore were so high and slender he was surprised she could walk on them, but she did fine. The long coils of ribbon trailed down the front of her, some reaching her waist. His gaze locked on the ones resting on her nipples. He glided his finger along one of the ribbons, then over her nub. It hardened under his touch.

He pulled his pocket knife from his pants and opened it, then cut through the ribbon attached to the collar and tossed the mass of curls aside. He dragged the back of the cold steel blade over her nub, watching her expression. The total trust in her eyes filled him with happiness. He closed the knife and put it away.

"You look amazing." Her hair was swept up but a few strands had escaped so he stroked them from her face. "I thought you'd forgotten my birthday."

She bit her lip and at her contrite expression, he regretted mentioning it.

"I did, sir. And I'm sorry. It was thoughtless of me." She turned and bent over just enough to push her ass toward him. "Please, sir. I should be punished."

Oh, God. The sight of her firm round ass sent heat flooding to his groin, but her begging him to punish her made his cock harden painfully.

His hand cupped her naked ass, the soft skin tempting him to do what he'd wanted to for so long. To smack that lovely flesh and watch it turn a deep rose.

"Yes, you deserve to be punished, but I'll decide when."

"Yes, Master Zane."

Her eyes were downturned, just as a good sub should do, but he tucked his hand under her chin and lifted until her gaze met his.

"You want to do this, Chelsea? To submit to my domination?"

Her eyes widened a little and he could see the nervousness there.

"I thought you would like it. I want to make your birthday special."

He smiled. "This will make it very special indeed… but only if you want it, too."

A deep hunger boiled in the depth of her gold-flecked brown eyes.

"I do." Her voice, hoarse and full of need, left no question in his mind.

"Kneel," he commanded.

She knelt down in front of him and he took her hand, then rested it on his painfully swollen cock.

"You see what you've done to me."

She ran her fingertips along his shaft and gazed up at him, nodding.

"What do you think you should do about it?"

She curled her hand around him through the fabric of his pants.

"Would you like me to relieve the pressure, Master Zane?"

She pulled down his zipper, then pressed her hand against his cock, the thin cotton fabric of his boxers between their naked skin.

"I would like that. But what I'd like more right now," he said as he stepped back, "is that you kneel down on the ground, face to the floor, and raise your ass in the air."

Her eyes widened and he thought for a moment she would refuse, but then she sank to the ground and pressed her hands and cheek to the floor. Then she pushed her ass upward. He walked around behind her and admired the view. He could see the small strip of her leather crotch which hid her intimate folds.

Was she wet?

He crouched behind her and ran his finger over the leather. Then he tugged on the snap holding the crotch to the waistband of the thong and drew the strip of leather away, revealing her glistening pink folds. He ran his finger along the tender flesh, loving the feel of her slickness. Yes, she was *very* wet. Then he glided a finger inside her. Then a second one.

He stroked her inside and she murmured softly.

"Do you like that, my little slave?"

"Yes, Master."

Hearing her call him Master exhilarated him. He pushed deeper into her, stroking her intimate passage. Then he stood up and dropped his pants and knelt behind her. He pulled her against his crotch, his hard cock straining against his boxers as her moistness seeped through the thin fabric. She surged back and ground her hips against him. He chuckled and eased her away, then pulled his cock free and glided the tip against her slit. Moving up and down her slickness as she moaned softly.

"Do you want me to fuck you, my slave? To drive my hard cock into you?"

"Yes, Master. Please."

He loved the need in her voice.

He pushed his cockhead into her. Just a little. Then he pulled it away, to her groan of disapproval.

He stood up and walked to the leather chair, then sat down.

"Come over here and suck my cock."

She stood up and walked toward him, then knelt in front of him. She wrapped her hand around his thick cock, still slick from her moisture, then leaned forward and took it into her mouth. He stifled his groan at the intensely exciting feel of her warm mouth surrounding him. Her lips squeezed him as she glided down his long shaft.

* * *

Chelsea couldn't believe she was doing this. Kneeling in front of her guardian, Zane, his thick erection in her mouth as she played the role of his slave. His cock was hot and smooth, the veins pulsing in her hand as she held him, her mouth gliding along his length.

God, her insides ached at the knowledge he would soon fuck her. His enormous cock driving deep into her. Filling her over and over again.

"Take it all the way down your throat, slave."

She relaxed her throat and took him deep, then glided back again. He surged forward, filling her throat, starting a slow and steady rhythm as he fucked her mouth. She cupped his balls and stroked, rewarded by his murmur of approval.

"Stroke your breast as you suck me," he commanded.

She cupped her breast as she squeezed his cock, then began to suck. Her fingertips found her nipple and she squeezed, then toyed with the hard nub, quivers of pleasure curling through her. He reached for her other breast and cupped it as she continued to suck. Then she felt him tense. His hand fell away and he arched forward. She could feel his balls tighten and then he groaned. Hot liquid flooded from his tip, filling her mouth.

She swallowed, not letting a single drop escape. When the flow ended, she eased away and ran her tongue around her lips. The heat in his eyes caused a slow burn inside her.

"You did very well my little slave. Now stand up."

She stood up, intensely aware of his hot gaze gliding the length of her essentially naked body.

"Show me your pussy. Open it to me."

She reached down, her cheeks flushing a little, and drew open the flesh so he could see her opening. He leaned forward and she almost squealed in delight as his tongue nudged against her flesh, then licked her. His hand cupped her ass and he drew her closer, then buried his face in her folds.

"Oh, yes," she whimpered.

He nuzzled and licked. His tongue swept over her clit. Then he teased in earnest. Intense pleasure coiled inside her and she moaned. It kept rising, pulsing through her, until she hovered near the edge of the precipice, knowing that wondrous pleasure was only a breath away.

She was so close.

Then he stopped.

"Noooo."

"Now it's time for that punishment."

He eased her back, then stood up and guided her to a bench. He leaned her over until her torso rested on the padded fabric, her bare ass toward him.

"Open your legs."

She widened her stance, baring her intimate flesh to him.

"Very nice." He stroked her naked ass, his hand caressing in circles.

Then he slapped her. The smack resounded through the room, and her flesh heated. Another stinging slap make her cry out.

"Do you like that?"

She didn't want to lie, but she wasn't sure and—

"Answer me, slave."

"I don't know, sir."

He swatted her ass again, but this time he stroked her intimate flesh afterward. She moaned at his caress.

Then she felt his cockhead nudge her opening. He pushed in, but only a little. She squeezed around him, trying to pull him deeper. He smacked her again, then slid his cockhead a little deeper.

“Oh, Master.”

He gave a quick smack to each cheek then pushed deeper.

“Do you want more?”

“Yes. Oh, please, yes.”

He slapped her burning flesh, sending ripples of pleasure through her as he glided deeper, her pussy sheathing more of his hard cock.

The pleasure and pain combined in an exhilarating rush of sensations. She wanted more. Of his cock driving into her. Of his hand searing across her ass.

His cock drove all the way inside, followed by a quick slap on each cheek. She moaned.

Then he drew out, slowly. Instead of driving deep again, he slipped free. But then she felt his cockhead nudge her back passage. She gasped and wanted to protest, but stopped herself.

She had given herself to Zane for his pleasure. And she trusted him.

He pushed forward, his cock stretching her tight opening.

He moved slowly and relentlessly, her ass opening around him. Hugging him tight. When his cockhead was fully immersed, he stopped, then stroked her burning ass cheek.

"Are you all right?" he asked.

"Yes, sir. Please fuck my ass."

* * *

Oh, God, hearing Chelsea say that drove Zane wild. He had to stop himself from driving deep into her in a single thrust. Instead, he slowly glided into her, her passage squeezing him tightly. The heady feel of her body gripping him like that made it hard to hold back, but he inched into her until finally, he was all the way inside.

He wrapped his arms around her waist and held her close.

"God, it feels so good being inside you like this."

"Thank you, Master Zane."

He laughed. "I can't tell you how much I like hearing you call me that. And 'sir' too. I think maybe we should make it a regular thing."

"Whatever you want, Master Zane. I am yours to command."

"God, baby, that is so fucking sexy."

"Master Zane, I need you so badly. Please make me come."

"Oh, fuck."

He glided his hand down her stomach to her folds and found her clit. He drew back, then glided deep into her ass again as he stroked the hard little nub. She arched back against him, pushing him deeper still. Making him groan.

He drew back and drove deep again, filling her with a slow, steady rhythm while he teased her clit. He was rewarded with the sound of her accelerated breathing.

“Are you close, little slave?”

“Oh, yes, Master,” she panted. “Please, sir. Make me come.”

Her words nearly drove him over the edge, pleasure swamping his senses, but he held back and drove hard and deep. Over and over again. She began to moan, setting his blood ablaze. He flicked her clit harder, driving into her faster.

She gasped, then her moans turned to shrill wails, filling the room with the sound of her pleasure.

Heat swelled in his groin, then it happened. His cock erupted inside her like a volcano, stealing his breath. He pumped and pumped, riding the wave of intense pleasure, then finally slumped on her back.

He rested against her, the two of them panting. Soon their breathing returned to normal, though he still floated on a wave of delight.

“Thank you, Master Zane.”

* * *

As Zane's joyous laugh filled the room, Chelsea smiled. His cock was still deep inside her and she squeezed.

"You're welcome, little slave, but my commands are not done yet."

A tremor of excitement danced along her spine.

"Of course, Master."

He stood up, drawing her upright with him. His hand stroked up her stomach, then cupped her breast for a quick caress.

"Stand at the wall, by the chains," he commanded.

She moved to the wall where he'd first taken her, excitement skittering through her. He disappeared into the washroom then returned totally naked. He moved like a panther as he approached her, his muscles rippling as he walked. To her surprise he stood with his back to the wall and lifted his arms. "Chain my wrists."

"But Master—"

"Are you refusing me?"

"No, sir, but I'm *yours* to command."

"And I'm commanding you to chain my wrists. Do it."

"Yes, sir."

She clamped a cuff around one wrist, then the other. He stood in front of her, in all his naked glory, essentially her prisoner.

Except they both knew the second he told her to unchain him she would.

"Now touch me."

"Where?" she asked.

He smiled. "Anywhere you want."

She gazed at his magnificent body. The desire to feel his solid muscles filled her. She rested her hand on his shoulder, then glided down his hard chest. Slowly, her fingertips grazed over his sculpted abs, then back up to his nipple. She toyed with it, loving the feel of the small bead under her fingertip. Then she glided downward again, the allure of his towering erection too much for her.

As soon as her finger brushed the tip, his cock twitched. She wrapped her hand around him and stroked his considerable length. She crouched down and gazed at his long, hard member close up as she stroked it up and down. Then she leaned forward and kissed the smooth shaft, near the base. His groan encouraged her and she lifted his balls in her hand then pressed her lips to them.

"God damn."

His strained, pleasure-filled voice made her smile. She opened her mouth and softly nibbled his shaven testicles. His cock lurched and heat surged through her at the thought of it inside her again. She drew his balls fully into her mouth and sucked softly, to his groan.

She stroked his thick cock and as her hand glided over his tip, she could feel the slickness of his precum.

“I want you to fuck me,” he said through gritted teeth.

She suckled deeply.

“Now, God damn it!”

Even though he was the one chained, his commanding tone made her jerk to her feet. She wrapped her hand around his shaft and tried to press it to her slick opening, but he was a little too tall for her. He bent his knees until she could press him against her slick flesh… then she eased closer, his cock sinking into her. Tears trickled from her eyes at the sheer pleasure of having him inside her. She pushed him deeper, her opening stretching around him.

He was so thick. So hard.

Finally, she had him all the way inside, their bodies tight together. She rested against him for a moment, enjoying the feel of his hard chest against her cheek, his heart thumping loudly. His erection inside her becoming the center of her being.

“Fuck me,” he snarled, his voice filled with need.

“Yes, Master,” she whispered.

She drew back, the agonizing feel of his cock dragging along her passageway sending need humming through her. Then she surged forward, taking him deep again.

"Fuck, unchain me."

Dazed by the intensity of the pleasure, she reached for his wrist.

"Now, damn it."

Worry filled her as she released one wrist. His arm curled around her as she released the other.

"Have I displeased you, M—"

He spun her around and rammed her against the wall, knocking the breath from her.

"Fuck, I need you so bad," he grated, his eyes filled with blazing desire.

Then he thrust deep into her. She gasped, then he drew out and thrust deep again, driving her against the cold, hard wall.

His lips found hers and his tongue drove deep as he thrust again. Pleasure swelled within her, and her intimate muscles gripped him as he drove in and out of her body. He grabbed her wrists and pushed them to the wall, holding her trapped.

"Tell me you want me," he insisted, his cock driving deep again.

She nodded, trying to find her voice.

"Yes, I want you." The words came out a hoarse whisper, then she whimpered as he drove deep again.

His lips captured hers again as he pumped deeper and harder. Joy rose in her.

"Tell me you love me."

The intensity of the sensations… the joyful surge of emotion… His thick shaft drove into her, filling her with bliss.

"Tell me," he insisted, his lips brushing her ear.

"I love you," she murmured, barely aware of the words she uttered, then plummeted over the edge. She strained against his hold, an orgasm bursting through her. Filling her with a joy like no other. Deep. Intense.

Soul-shattering.

He thrust deep and groaned. The feel of him erupting inside her sent her head spinning and she wailed as another orgasm exploded inside her.

She leaned against him, her head resting on his shoulder, as they both gasped for breath. After a moment, he lifted her into his arms and carried her upstairs.

* * *

The warm water of the shower washed over Chelsea's body as Zane rubbed a bar of soap between his hands, then put it down and stroked over her body, washing her. His big hands moved over her breasts then down her stomach.

She simply watched him. His naked body so large and masculine seemed to fill the shower stall. She sighed as his sudsy hands glided over her like silk.

"Why did you tell me to say that?" she asked, the thing that had been bothering her finally breaking through to her consciousness.

"Say what?" His hands glided over her breasts again.

"Why did you tell me to say I love you?"

He stopped the distracting movement of his hands and straightened. "Because I wanted to hear you say it." He cupped her chin and lifted her face, his clear blue gaze locked on hers. "I wanted you to know it's true."

Her stomach fluttered. He was so sure.

"But… you didn't say it, too."

His serious expression softened with his smile.

He slid his arm around her and drew her close. His lips brushed hers, lightly at first, then he deepened the kiss, claiming her mouth as completely as he'd claimed her heart.

"Of course I love you," he murmured, then kissed her again, his tongue swirling in her mouth, making her knees grow weak.

Their lips parted and his deep blue eyes held her mesmerized.

"Do you really have any doubts?"

She could see it there in his eyes, shining bright. She shook her head.

He smiled. “Good.” Then he slapped her ass lightly. He picked up the soap and handed it to her, then stepped back. “Now you have some washing to do.”

She ran her gaze up and down his deliciously naked body. “But mine is such a bigger job than yours.”

He chuckled, his eyes glittering in amusement. But when she soaped up her hands and stroked down his chest, then wrapped both hands around his cock that glitter changed to something else. The flesh hardened in her hand and soon she knew he would back her against the wall and drive deep inside her.

* * *

Chelsea stepped from the gate into the boarding area, rolling her carry-on behind her. It had been a long flight from New York to San Diego and she was tired. She had to get a cab home and unpack, then catch up on her emails, but she just wanted to fall into bed. She sighed, already missing Zane. The memory of the kiss he’d given her as he’d bid her farewell at the airport still curled her toes. He’d promised he’d come to visit her soon but until then she’d be aching for him.

The security doors slid open as she approached and she walked into the busy terminal.

When she saw Bill waiting for her, she smiled.

“Hi. I didn’t expect you to pick me up.”

“It’s no problem. Did you have a good flight?” he asked as he walked with her to the baggage carousel.

“A little bumpy but other than that it was fine.”

The carousel was already turning, with several bags already being claimed by passengers. After a few moments, she saw her red bag glide down the ramp. She retrieved it then Bill took the handle and they walked through the airport together. When they finally reached his car, he loaded her luggage into his trunk and they both got in.

“Are you hungry?” he asked. “I thought we might go to dinner.”

“To tell you the truth, I’m beat. I just want to go home and go to sleep.” It was still early evening, but she was still on New York time.

“Okay.” He started the car and pulled out. “So how did your trip go? Did you talk about your company with your guardian?”

This morning at breakfast, Zane had made some interesting revelations. Like the fact that he had implemented many of the ideas she had suggested. In fact, he’d done them better than she’d thought possible. Her biggest concern had been environmental issues—making No Limits a greener company—but the suggestions she'd made hadn't been practical. Zane had taken her ideas and sought out innovative solutions to accomplish the same goals.

If she had paid more attention to the reports he'd sent her over the past couple of years, she would have known he'd been trying to incorporate her ideas. In fact, he'd told her years ago that he would do what he could, but she'd taken that as a brush off. She'd become disheartened and decided it was better not to care than to fight.

"Zane and I did have some interesting discussions. He's actually made some big steps toward making No Limits environmentally friendly."

"That's great."

She glanced at Bill as he drove. Neither his face nor his voice convinced her he actually thought it was great.

"Do you have something on your mind?" she asked, concerned he was worried about some problem at work. "You seem preoccupied."

"No." He smiled, shooting a quick glance her way. "I'm glad you had a good visit. I'm just a bit surprised. I thought you and Zane didn't get along, but then you spent the weekend with him and now it feels as if things are good between you."

His concern surprised her, and disturbed her a little. She wasn't sure why, but just a feeling. Was it because he sensed that her relationship with Zane had made a fundamental shift? Was it possible that the fact that she was in love with Zane showed all over her face? She wasn't quite ready for the world to know. She was still getting used to the fact herself. But would Bill judge her?

Or was her niggling worry that he wanted to start a relationship with her actually true? Bill was a great guy, but she just didn't think of him that way. If he had hoped for a romantic relationship, however, that could make for problems.

"Yes, things are a lot better between us. But don't worry. I'm not about to abandon Quiet Thunder."

He frowned. "No, of course not. I never thought you would."

But for some reason, his words and his demeanor didn't seem to match.

He pulled in front of her apartment and she got out. He fetched her luggage from the trunk.

"You sure about dinner? Even a coffee?" he asked as he rolled her suitcase to the door.

"No, I'm really beat."

"Okay. Uh… just so you know… A board meeting has been called and it's on for tomorrow afternoon."

"What? Why didn't I know about this?"

"It happened last week, but I thought you'd be back on Friday." He shrugged. "I didn't want to bother you on your weekend away."

"What's being discussed at the meeting?"

"We can talk about that tomorrow."

She was about to protest, but he'd already turned to walk back to his car. She wasn't happy that he'd withheld the information. He may have meant well, knowing she'd stress about it, but she didn't like being kept in the dark.

When she finally reached her apartment, she dragged her luggage into the bedroom, then shed her clothes and climbed into bed. As tired as she was, though, sleep did not come. Even thoughts of Zane and the wonderful, life-changing weekend they'd spent together, wasn't enough to distract her from the worry of this sudden meeting.

* * *

Chelsea walked into the office the next day a bit bleary-eyed. She hadn't slept well and she was concerned.

"Where's Bill?" she asked when she saw Sandy.

"He's out at a meeting with a new client all morning."

Chelsea frowned. "We were supposed to talk about the board meeting this afternoon. What can you tell me about it?"

"Sorry, I don't know anything about it. I didn't even hear about it until yesterday and Bill just asked me to set up the boardroom for it. Why? Do you think there's some problem?"

"No, I'm sure it's nothing major," she lied. She didn't want Sandy worried about her job.

As she walked back to her office, she sucked in a breath. She was overreacting. Ever since they went public and had to have a board oversee the company, she'd felt like there was someone looking over her shoulder, but everything had been fine. Most of the board meetings were actually pretty mundane.

She went through her emails and got caught up on a few outstanding issues, then she went and talked to Dan in research about a problem with the newest battery they were adding to their product line. They already had a lot of interest from a couple of the major cell phone companies.

The morning slipped by, which always happened when she was able to roll up her sleeves and get involved in the design process, something that rarely happened now that the company had grown to over forty people and Bill insisted the two of them needed to lead, not just work in the trenches. But being an engineer was her passion, as it had been with her parents.

Her cell phone rang and she picked it up.

"Hey, it's Sandy. Where are you? The meeting starts in ten minutes."

Chelsea glanced at her watch. “Oh, damn. I’ll be right up.”

She’d totally lost track of the time, missing lunch entirely. Dan thanked her—they’d gotten past his initial problem and had made headway in resolving a new issue that had arisen.

She hurried to the elevator, catching it just as the door was closing. When the doors whooshed open, she walked to the boardroom, drawing in deep, calming breaths. She could see through the glass that the board members were already seated at the large, glossy mahogany table. She saw Bill walking down the hall toward the room.

“Bill, we never got a chance to talk this morning. Do you want to fill me in on what’s going on?”

His lips compressed. “Maybe we should just get in there.”

But there were unfamiliar faces in the room and that made her nervous.

“Not until you tell me what the meeting is about and who those two men are.”

Bill glanced to the two well-dressed strangers sitting at the board table.

“All right. There’s no easy way to tell you this, but…I received an offer to buy the company.”

“But we don’t want to sell.”

“No. *You* don’t want to sell. I do. And I have the support of the major investors.”

Her eyes widened. “You talked to them?”

The cool, determined look in his eyes was her answer.

“Look, Chelsea, this is not a bad thing. We’re going to make a shitload of money on this deal.”

Her fists clenched. “I don’t care about the money.”

“Well, I do, and this time you don’t get the final say.”

The final say? In her whole life, when had she ever gotten the final say?

He gripped her arm. “Come on. We’ve got a meeting to attend.”

She tugged her arm free. “And what if I don’t go?”

He shrugged. “That’s your choice, but we’ll have quorum without you. I’ve ensured that our silent partner and a representative from the company that owns the majority of the public shares will be present. We have a majority vote without you.”

Bill turned and walked into the boardroom and sat down at the table. Chelsea followed him and sank down in a chair.

The chairman started the meeting and went through the usual review of the past minutes, et cetera. Chelsea barely heard what they were saying over the pounding of her heart. Then her breath caught when he announced that an offer had been made on the company.

Bill was called up to explain the offer. After this, the chairman would call for a vote and, if Bill truly did have the support of the investors, she was screwed. She, Bill, and the angel investor had twenty percent each, and the other forty percent were publicly traded shares. She knew that almost half of those shares were owned by one company, a fact that had always made her a little nervous, but not as much as now when she knew that Bill, the angel investor and that other company owned enough shares for a majority vote.

Oh, God, she was going to lose the company.

"Are we ready to vote?" the chairman asked when Bill finished speaking.

"Wait." The tall stranger in the navy suit stood up. "I just received word that the owner of my firm wants to be present for the vote personally. He's at reception."

Bill stood up. "I'll bring him in." Then he disappeared out the door.

The tension was unbearable as Chelsea sat waiting for her world to crumble beneath her. Finally, she stood up and walked out of the room, determined to do something. She walked down the hall then turned toward the reception area

Then she saw him. Zane standing talking to Bill.

But Bill had never met Zane before. Why would he…?

Then Bill shook Zane's hand.

"I'm glad you're on board," Bill said. "It's a good offer."

Her heart sank. *Oh, my God. Zane is the other major stockholder.*

She pushed aside the shock. With everything that had happened between them on the weekend, he must have bought the shares to protect her. He was here to help. Somehow, he would make it all right. She knew it in her heart.

"You will be voting with me?" Bill asked.

"Of course," Zane said. "As you say, it's an excellent offer."

Chelsea sucked in a breath. Her heart compressed and she felt nauseous. Zane was betraying her.

Zane glanced in her direction.

"Chelsea."

"You know each other?" Bill asked in surprise.

But Chelsea ignored him. "I can't believe you would do this." Anger seared through her. "That you would betray me like this…" Oh, God, her voice was shaking. She couldn't… she *wouldn't* let him see her tears.

She turned and hurried down the side corridor toward the elevator, racing past Sandy, then jabbed at the elevator button.

"Hey, Chelsea, you're white as a ghost. Everything okay?" Sandy asked.

Chelsea just shook her head, relieved when the elevator doors opened and she stepped inside, then pushed the button to close the doors. But her heart sank even more when she realized Zane wasn't following her.

Oh, God, had last week and this weekend been all about keeping her preoccupied so she didn't know what Bill was up to? Everything Zane had said he felt for her…she realized now it had all been a lie.

* * *

Chelsea flinched at the pounding on her apartment door. Zane had texted to say he was on his way over, and someone must have let him in the front door.

"Chelsea, let me in," he said in exasperation, the knocking getting louder.

She'd been refusing to acknowledge him for a good ten minutes, but clearly he wasn't going to give up. She walked to the door and turned the lock.

When she opened the door, the sight of his handsome, determined face threw her totally off balance.

"I don't want to talk to you."

He pushed past her. "We're going to talk about this."

She closed the door and turned to him. "There's nothing you can say—"

"That's not true. Now come and sit down."

She walked into the living room but refused to sit. Tears welled from her eyes and all the things she'd wanted to say to him over the past hour…all the pain he had caused her… bubbled to the surface.

"I don't understand how you could…" Her throat tightened, choking off the words.

She drew in a breath, trying to calm herself. "When I was younger, I trusted you. Then our parents died and you turned into my father and never listened to me or cared what I wanted. But then… this weekend… you turned everything around. You convinced me you …" She choked up again. She sucked in a deep, wobbly breath. "You convinced me you were in love with me."

"I am."

"Not just you loving me like someone you're obligated to take care of..." she continued, ignoring him.

"That's not—"

"But like you were *really* in love with me."

"Chelsea—"

She turned her back on him and walked to the window, unable to look at him anymore.

She felt him approach and wanted to stride away. To get as far from him as she could. But her legs wouldn't move. If she forced them, she knew she'd stumble.

His hand rested on her shoulder.

"Chelsea," he said softly. "I do love you. With all my heart."

She spun around, glaring at him with a ferocity that shocked her. "And that's how you show it? By working with my partner to sell my company out from under me?"

"That's not what happened."

"I just talked to Sandy. She told me about the vote."

"She wasn't in the meeting. Please, let me explain."

"No!" She marched away, forcing her legs to move. One step after another. Propelling her away from him.

Just as she reached the door, ready to exit the apartment, he spoke.

"Chelsea, stop." He used that tone. The one that reached inside her somehow and compelled her to do what he said.

She hesitated, her hand hovering on the door knob.

"I didn't take your company away from you. I worked against your son-of-a-bitch partner."

A hand squeezed around her heart, accelerating her breathing. Could it be true?

She turned slowly.

His somber blue gaze locked on hers. He was telling the truth. She knew he was.

He'd never lied to her. He always told her the truth, even if it wasn't what she wanted to hear.

But it wasn't like him to take the losing side of a battle.

"So you came here to vote even though you knew we couldn't win?"

Her twenty percent and his fifteen wouldn't beat the combined twenty plus twenty shares of Bill and the angel investor.

"Why do you think we didn't win?"

Hope fluttered inside her but… she didn't understand.

"I…" She shook her head. He knew the math as well as her. "Bill said he had the support of the angel investor." She wanted to grab onto the hope Zane offered and cling to it, but she knew better. "An angel investor wants to prosper from his investment and from the offer Bill received. No sane investor would say no." Only someone like her, who was passionate about the company… who had pride in having built it from her own ideas and vision… would keep it in the face of an offer like that. "He'd have to be an idiot to turn it down."

His lips quirked up. "I don't think of myself as an idiot."

She shook her head. "What?"

He stepped closer, then took her hand in his. It was so warm, his fingers enveloping her cold ones.

"I said I'm not an idiot. I'm the one who invested in your company when you were starting out. Through a separate corporation so you wouldn't know."

Her eyes widened.

"And before you go there, it wasn't to keep any kind of control over you. I knew how much you wanted this. I wanted to make sure that no one could ever take it away from you." He squeezed her hand. "Ever."

"You…" Her throat was so tight the word sounded strangled. She tried again. "You're the investor? You…voted against Bill?"

He smiled and drew her toward him. "You didn't really think I'd ever let anyone hurt you like that, did you?"

He pulled her into his arms and held her tight. Her head rested against the smooth wool of his suit, her tears dampening the fabric.

He had saved her company.

"Sweetheart, I love you. I have always done whatever I can to protect you. You may have felt it was controlling, but…" His lips brushed against her temple. "I could just never stand to see you hurt."

She eased back and stared up at him as she blinked back the tears.

"So Sandy was wrong? The company is not being sold?"

He tipped his head. "No, she's not wrong. The company is being sold. To me."

Her gut reaction was to push him away, assuming he was taking control. That his attitude was that she'd had her chance to run a company… and failed. Now he'd take over and do what she couldn't.

But he deserved better than that. This weekend had changed everything she thought she'd known about him.

He smiled. "When I heard via my sources that Bill had received an offer for the company, I had one of my subordinate companies make a better offer. He was chomping at the bit to get his hands on all that money. It was clear that he doesn't have the same love of this company as you do. He knew you'd never go for it, so he decided to get your angel investor on-board, not knowing it was me. I instructed my representative to let him believe I was on board. He also reached out to other big investors, intent on getting a majority vote. I already had an extra chunk of stock I'd bought and when I saw what he was doing, I bought more."

"Why did you have extra stock?" She didn't want to believe it was because he wanted control.

He laughed and stroked her cheek. "Because, sweetheart, I believe in you. I *knew* your company was a good investment."

Hearing him say those words made her heart swell. *He believes in me.* Tears started to flow again.

"But, you know, I don't see why you need a partner. Especially one who doesn't share your passion. So I did buy the company. Bill will get his money, and so will the other investors. Your company will be privately owned again."

"By you."

He shook his head. "No. By you. The company will flourish with you at the helm. I've already signed the papers transferring ownership to you."

"You're giving me the company?"Joyful relief surged through her.

He nodded.

"You can't just give it to me. You invested the majority of the money."

"And you invested your heart." He tipped her chin up and kissed her. "It's yours."

Her heart soared. He did believe in her.

And he did love her. He'd just proven that.

He knew she was strong and capable and he was willing to put a huge amount of money behind that belief.

She shook her head. "No. I think it should be fifty-fifty."

"Yeah? Why is that?"

She rested her hand on his cheek. "Because I think that's how it should be between a husband and wife."

She nearly laughed out loud at the shock in his eyes.

"Are you saying…?"

She took his hand as she sank to her knees. "Zane, I love you with all my heart. I know you will always care for me and protect me. I know I can trust you with my life." She smiled. "And I've learned a lot about how to give up control after this past weekend. So I want to spend my life obeying you." She stared straight into his steady blue gaze. "Will you marry me?"

He chuckled and pulled her to her feet and straight into his arms. His tongue delved deep, claiming her with a passion that took her breath away. When he released her mouth, she could barely breathe.

"Yes."

It was her turn to laugh, then she threw her arms around him and hugged him tight, her heart pounding in her chest.

His hand stroked down her back and over her ass, then he pulled her tight to him. The hard bulge against her belly told her he'd missed her as much as she'd missed him. She knelt down again, stroking her hand from his chest to his growing cock. The feel of his hard shaft beneath the fine wool of his suit pants sent her heart racing. She unzipped him and pulled out his big, pulsing cock, already steel-hard with wanting her. She smiled as she admired his length, her hand stroking slowly from base to tip.

She gazed up at him. “What would you like me to do, Master Zane?”

“You’ve just become head of your own company.” He smiled. “I’d like you to take control.”

She stood up. “Really?”

She stepped back, unbuttoning her blouse as her gaze glided up and down his body. His swollen cock twitched under her scrutiny. She dropped her blouse to the floor and ran her fingertips over the swell of her breasts, watching his eyes darken.

“I want you naked,” she said.

“Yes, Mistress,” he said as he took off his suit jacket.

She watched hungrily as he unfastened the buttons of his shirt, one-by-one, slowly revealing his broad chest. The first peek at his sculpted abs sent her heart pumping faster. He shed his shirt, then unfastened the button of his pants—she’d already undone the zipper. He pushed them down, along with his underwear, and stepped out of them. Then he stood up. Fully and gloriously naked.

Heat hummed through her at the sight of him. So incredibly masculine. So strong and dominant. Yet willing to give control to her.

She reached around behind her and unfastened her skirt, then pushed it to the floor.

“What would you like to do to me?” she asked coyly.

“Whatever will make you happy, Mistress.”

“Then come here and take off my bra.”

As he stepped closer, her heart-rate increased. His arms went around her and his fingers played along her back, then the bra released. He eased the straps from her shoulders, the feel of his fingertips brushing her skin sending tingles dancing along her flesh. Then he drew the bra from her breasts, revealing them.

Her nipples puckered at his heated gaze.

“You are beautiful, Mistress. What would you like me to do now?”

“I want you to caress my breasts.”

He enveloped her breasts in his hands, then stroked her nipples with his thumbs, until they were hard and needy.

“Take one in your mouth,” she murmured.

His head dipped down then she felt moistness encompass her hard nub as he wrapped his lips around it. He nudged it with his tongue, then sucked softly. She groaned at the exquisite sensations. He moved to her other breast, suckling it until she could barely stand.

"Take off my panties." Her hoarse voice reflected her need.

He drew them down, his hot gaze lingering on her pussy.

"I want you to touch me… lick me…" she ran her fingers down her stomach then over her slick folds. "Here."

She moved to the couch and sat down, opening her legs wide to him.

He smiled as he knelt in front of her. "Of course, Mistress."

The first touch of his fingers sent a jolt of pleasure through her. Heat blossomed inside her as his fingers glided over her intimate flesh. Then he leaned forward and when his tongue touched her, she moaned. He lapped over her sensitive flesh, then nuzzled in deep. Her fingers curled around his head, gliding through the thick waves of his hair.

Pulling him closer. He lifted his head and she groaned.

"Would you like me to make you come, Mistress?"

"Oh, yes. Please."

He chuckled. His fingers stroked her slit, then one glided inside. His talented tongue found her clit and he swirled over it. Another finger slid inside her and he stroked her passage. Pleasure washed through her. Then he began to suckle her clit and it flared to joyous abandon as she gave herself over to him. His fingers glided in and out of her as his mouth mastered her clitoris, driving her joy higher and higher. She pulled his head tighter to her as she rode the wave to new heights. Ecstatic waves of divine bliss pummeled her until she moaned in release.

He continued to stroke and suckle until finally the orgasm relented, leaving her breathlessly draped against the couch.

He stared at her, a warm smile on his face.

"Oh, God, I'll never get enough of that," she admitted.

"Well, if Mistress wishes…" And he leaned forward again.

She laughed, pressing her hand to his shoulder to stop him. Then she pulled him in for a kiss. His lips met hers, brushing softly, then he deepened the kiss. He was leaning over her, his knees against the couch, and she could feel his hard, thick cock brushing her stomach.

And she wanted it inside so much. She could just wrap her hand around it and position it against her, then he would drive forward, filling her with his thick shaft.

But not yet. She wanted… something…

She nuzzled her lips along his cheek to his ear, then murmured, "Stand up."

He stood, then offered her hand and pulled her to her feet.

They stood facing other, her breasts almost brushing his chest. She closed the distance, her hard nipples pressing against him, and grasped his shoulders.

"I want you to smack my bottom."

He smacked, sending a burning heat across her skin.

"Again."

She moaned at the feel of his hand connecting with her ass.

"Again", she insisted, as she ground against him, feeling his steel hard rod digging into her flesh.

He smacked again and she moaned.

She turned around, moved behind the armchair and leaned over, exposing her ass to him.

"Now I want you to spank me as you push your cock into me."

The glint in his eye as he walked toward her sent her insides fluttering.

He stepped behind her and she felt his hand stroke over her burning ass. Then the tip of his hot, thick cockhead pressed against her slick flesh. He eased forward, just a bit, his thick cockhead stretching her. Slowly, he moved forward until his bulbous head was nestled inside her. She sucked in a breath at his stinging slap on her left cheek, followed by a quick slap on the right.

He smacked her bottom a few more times as his thick cock stretched her on its journey inside. Filling her. When he was all the way inside her, she arched against him. He pressed her cheeks together, squeezing her passage tighter around his solid shaft.

"Oh, God… fuck me!"

He laughed joyously, then drew back, still holding her cheeks together, augmenting the feel of his cockhead dragging along her tight passage.

Then he drove deep again. Tingling sensations swamped her with joy and she gasped.

He drew out and thrust in.

Yes… please…" she begged, needing the pleasure only he could give her.

He filled her again and again. Pleasure swirled through her, rising higher and higher. His thick shaft stroked her. In and out. A blissful sensation flickered in her core, then expanded, swelling through her whole body.

"Zane. Yes. Oh, God, yes…you're making me come."

He moved faster. His relentless cock driving into her set her body ablaze, igniting the joy until it exploded in a soul-shattering orgasm.

She wailed her release as he pounded into her, then he ground deep and she felt his hot seed erupt inside her. Finally, he collapsed on her back, his arms around her waist, the chair supporting them.

"Oh, my God, that was sensational." Then she found herself giggling.

He stood up, drawing her with him, then turned her around to face him.

"I will never control you, even if you're obeying me. I want you to understand that. And you can take the lead anytime you want. I will willingly submit to you."

She smiled. "Yes, I rather liked that."

His eyebrow arched. "So now am I the slave and you're the Mistress?"

She dragged a finger down his hard chest. "Sometimes that's fun. But I do so love when you dominate me. So don't think you're off the hook for that." Especially now that she knew how much he loved her, and that she could trust him completely.

"So be it. So as your Master, I will set the date for our wedding sometime next month and decide on a small gathering—"

"Now wait a minute. Maybe we'll just set some guidelines right now. I would like a large, fancy wedding with lots of guests."

"So you want to be totally in charge of the wedding?"

"No, you can help with it, but I will be the one in charge." She raised an eyebrow. "Do you have any problem with that?"

He laughed, then kissed her soundly. "None whatsoever."

"Good. I think this partnership is starting off very well."

"I agree." He scooped her up and carried her to the bedroom. "And I think we should seal it with something much more interesting than a handshake."

She laughed, her arms around his neck. "Didn't we just do that?"

"With something as important as a lifetime partnership, I think we should be really sure we're in full agreement."

He laid her on the bed and prowled over her. As his already hard cock pushed into her, sending scintillating pleasure through her, she realized that everything she had ever wanted had just come true. As he thrust into her and her pleasure blossomed, she knew that they would always be this happy.

Because Zane loved her. And she loved him. Forever.

# # #

More by Opal Carew

If you enjoyed this story, you'll love Opal's next story in the Mastered By series, which you can find at **OpalCarew.com/bookshelf**

To hear about Opal's latest releases, sign up for her newsletter at **OpalCarew.com/newsletter**

You can keep in touch using the following links:

Website: **OpalCarew.com**
Newsletter: **OpalCarew.com/newsletter**
Facebook: **facebook.com/OpalCarewRomanceAuthor**
Twitter: **@opalcarew**
Pinterest: **pinterest.com/opalcarew/**
Smashwords: **smashwords.com/profile/view/OpalCarew**
Blog: **opalcarewromanceauthor.wordpress.com**

Excerpts

If you would like to read more Opal Carew stories, here are some recommendations. For more hot BDSM stories, try **Played By the Master**, **His To Possess**, or **Stepbrother, Mine**.

If you enjoy short, quick reads, Opal recommends her **Office Slave Series**, currently consisting of **The Office Slave**, **The Boss**, and **On Her Knees**. The first two stories are available at a significant discount in **The Office Slave Series, Book 1 & 2 Box Set**.

If you like rough and ready tattooed bikers who love to share their women, you will probably really enjoy her **Ready To Ride** biker erotic romance series, which consists of **Hot Ride** (novella), **Wild Ride** (novella), **Riding Steele** (novel) and **Hard Ride** (novel). These can each be read independently, but Opal recommends the above order.

Here are short excerpts from **Played By The Master, The Office Slave** and **Stepbrother, Mine**...

Played By The Master

by Opal Carew

Jacqueline crashes a billionaire's exclusive poker game in order to seduce him into a favor to save her sister, but instead finds herself played by the Master.

Jacqueline Bell desperately wants to help her sister out of a jam. But to do that, she has to find a way to talk to billionaire entrepreneur Race Danner, and have him drop the charges against her brother-in-law. She discovers he holds an exclusive poker game once a week and finds a way in.

Race Danner is bored with his life, despite his wealth and extreme hobbies. He doesn't know exactly what he's looking for, but he'll know it when he sees it.

When Jacqueline Bell walks into his life, he knows she's it. She wants something from him. And he wants her. A combination made in heaven. In a delicious game of cat and mouse, he will leverage his advantage to lure her into his game. And he fully intends to win.

Warning: This story has Domination, submission, bondage, punishment, and a lot of other fun things, plus explicit, wild sexual encounters. After all, if you're going to play, play hard! ;) Her ultimate sexual fantasy brought to life...

Excerpt

He smiled and at the predatory look in his eyes, Jacquie realized he was going to win. The blood drained from her face as he flipped over his cards… revealing a full house.

Oh, God, she'd lost her opportunity to try and convince him to help Ella and her husband.

"Come over here." His silken voice curled through her and she stood up.

Now he would touch her… probably cup her ass with his big hand. Maybe, if she seemed willing…who was she kidding, she *was* willing… to succumb to his touch, then maybe he would listen to her after all.

Shock vaulted through her at her own illicit thoughts. She wasn't going to sleep with him to help Ella.

No, just strip down to practically nothing. Then let him touch her.

Did she really know where her boundaries were?

He watched as she walked around the long table, then approached him, his gaze locked on the swell of her breasts above the lace cups. Her nipples puckered at the thought of him stroking her there.

He pushed his chair back from the table and turned sideways as she continued toward him. His intense male gaze sent heat shimmering through her.

Finally, she stood facing him.

He lifted his hand, and as it approached her, she calmed her breathing, readying herself for his touch. It would only be a moment.

But she wasn't prepared for the spark of desire that flared through her when his fingertips brushed against her skin, just above her elbow. Then his fingers moved. Upward. Trailing lightly over her shoulder, then down. She drew in a slow breath as he glided over the soft exposed skin of her breast, right to the lace of her bra. His fingertip grazed lightly under the scalloped edges, but not breaching the barrier of the satin cup.

Clearly, he liked to push boundaries.

And she was close to pulling back that boundary, by tugging forward the cup and inviting him to explore further. The thought of his big fingers gliding over her hard nipple sent her pulse fluttering.

Her own potent reaction to him startled her and she stepped back.

"I… uh… we're done now."

He arched an eyebrow. "I don't think so."

"You said a touch," she stammered.

"And you didn't say how long. I'm not finished."

"Well, I—"

"Come here," he said, his authoritative tone brooking no argument.

She stepped close again, shocking herself at her own submissiveness.

"So I just have to stand here for as long as you want to touch me?"

He gazed at her, his blue eyes twinkling. "Yes."

His fingers brushed her ribs this time, below her breast, then glided slowly downward, leaving a trail of goose bumps in their wake. She tried to ignore the heady sensations fluttering through her.

"But you could go on for hours."

He grinned. "Yes."

Oh, God, if he did this for even ten more minutes, she'd be a puddle on the ground.

The Office Slave

by Opal Carew

Her ultimate sexual fantasy brought to life…

Sylvia loves to read erotica, and after her latest read, she's developed a sizzling fantasy about being forced to submit to the sexual whims of four incredibly hot business partners. Never in her wildest dreams did she think she'd have the opportunity to live out her fantasy... until her friend decides to make it happen. Now she's about to become an office slave… to four hunky men she's never even met. But faced with the reality, can she actually go through with it?

Excerpt

Sylvia walked to the entrance and opened the glass door, then crossed the lobby, her high heels clicking on the marble floor. She glanced at the directory near the elevators, then walked down the hall to the end and stopped at Suite 105. A sign said to ring the bell, which she did. Becca had told her that these four men ran a software business, programming games.

This office was where they developed the games. Also, Becca had told her the guys were extremely good-looking. All but one of the men used to work with Cal as strippers before they graduated from college and started this business, so she didn't doubt it.

The door opened and she gazed up at a totally hot hunk wearing a suit, his long, black hair tied back. He had startling blue eyes that twinkled when he smiled at her.

"Are you Sylvia?"

She nodded.

He pulled the door open. "Please come in."

She stepped into the office. There was a large table in the center of an open space with a big window overlooking the city below and several doors to offices along the wall behind it. There was a hallway off to the side. The space had a lot of character, with red brick walls and a curved arch around the window.

"I'm Mike Bairn. Come on into my office."

She followed him across the central area to the leftmost office. One man was working in the far right office, but he didn't glance up.

"Am I early?" she asked as she sat down in the chair across from his desk.

"No, not at all. The others will meet us in the conference room in a few minutes."

She nodded, starting to feel a little nervous. Would her fantasy begin in the conference room? Would they order her to take off all her clothes, then… other things. She'd been looking forward to this fantasy for over a week—ever since Becca had told her she wanted to set it up, and that it would be acted out by some of Cal's ex-stripper friends—but now that the reality was here, she had a case of nerves.

This man Mike was extremely masculine, and sexy, and he set her hormones humming, but could she really just strip down and become his sex toy. Along his three partners, too?

Don't freak out now. This is your fantasy!

Mike leaned forward, his hands folded on his desk. "So Cal told us what you were looking for. As I understand it, your brother cheated us out of a sizeable amount of money and you agree to be our sex slave in return for not prosecuting him."

Sylvia felt her cheeks heat as she nodded. In her head, especially after reading that book, it seemed extremely sexy, but laid out blatantly like that made her feel brash and… well, maybe a little slutty. And… maybe she was being… uh…brash. But both Becca and Jan had lived out their fantasies, and both were pretty wild. Why shouldn't she?

And when she'd become enamored of the fantasy, she'd never, *ever* dreamed she'd live it out. What woman did? But now that she had the opportunity, she really didn't want to walk away.

"So, don't get me wrong, I find the whole thing wildly sexy, but…"—he shrugged—"we sound a bit mean, prosecuting your brother." At his grin and the twinkle in his eye, she knew he wasn't making fun of her, but he *was* teasing her.

"Well, he did do you wrong."

"True. But then we're distracted by a beautiful woman."

Her cheeks burned hotter at his compliment. "Well, a woman offering sex, anyway."

He chuckled and stood up. "Okay, I think we're ready to proceed. The others know the story and are ready to go and we all know the safe word is Tiger. The minute we step out of this office, we're into our roles. Okay?"

"Okay." Her stomach quivered as she stood up.

They walked to the door together, but before he opened it, he took her hand and kissed it. Tingles danced along her skin at the delicate brush of his lips.

"Sylvia, thank you for including us in your fantasy." Then he winked and opened the door.

She followed him to the end of the big table in the open area where he gestured for her to sit down. He tapped something on his phone, then leaned back in his chair.

"The others will be here in a few moments." His tone was more business-like now, rather than the easy banter of before.

The man from the other office walked to the chair next to Mike's and sat down, glancing at her speculatively. He had short cropped, sandy hair, a wide face with a square jaw, and warm, brown eyes. He wore dark blue jeans and a shirt. A moment later, two men appeared from the hallway, and Sylvia's breath caught at the side of the tall biker named Slade she'd seen entering the building earlier. Man, this fantasy was getting better by the minute. And the man by his side was the cyclist he'd spoken with at the door.

The cyclist's short, straight hair was a little damp—he'd probably taken a shower—and he wore dress pants and a striped shirt, accentuating his narrow waist and broad shoulders. Thoughts of him naked in the shower, water sluicing over his muscular body sent a quiver through her. Her gaze shifted to Slade, still wearing his jeans and T-shirt. Clearly, he was the rebel of the bunch.

They sat down and she glanced around the table at these four men, who used to be male strippers. They were all gorgeous and soon she'd be having hot, kinky sex with them all.

"This is Sylvia, the woman we discussed a few days ago. She's here because of the arrangement to compensate for her brother's debt," Mike said. "Sylvia, this is Granger Smith, Neil Craig, and Slade Forrester."

She nodded as she gazed at their serious expressions. Tension curled inside her.

"So, she's going to be our office slave, right?" Slade said.

"Yes, that's the arrangement," Mike answered.

"Good, then I think we should start right off with seeing what's underneath those clothes she's wearing.

Her gaze locked on his and his charcoal eyes glittered as a slow smile spread across his face. Heat washed through her.

"Excellent idea." Mike said.

Stepbrother, Mine

Opal Carew

When she was just sixteen, Dana found herself torn from her familiar life. Her mother had just remarried, and Dana was dragged to an elegant mansion where she spent most of her time alone while her mother traveled. No one seemed to care she was alive... until her older stepbrother moved in. Mason became her friend and protector. He brought light to her dark existence. But soon, to her dismay, she found that her heart raced and inappropriate feelings surged every time he was near. Then one day, as quickly as he'd come into her life, Mason disappeared again, leaving her more alone than she'd ever felt before.

Mason hated walking away from Dana all those years ago, but he had no choice. Leaving freed him from the devastating struggle against his own intense desire. Now the head of his own corporate empire, Mason has wealth, power, and no shortage of beautiful women ready to fulfill his every need. But despite having it all, Mason is bored. He's never forgotten Dana, even though she's the one woman in the world who is totally off-limits.

When he finds out she's in desperate need of money and has decided to auction off her virginity, Mason is unwilling to let Dana slip away again...even if it means bidding on the one thing that's always been completely forbidden.

Excerpt

"We're here, miss."

The driver stopped the car and got out, then opened her door and helped her from the car. They stood in front of a tall, elegant looking building. It didn't look like a hotel. More like a luxury apartment building. The driver rolled her overnight bag to the front door and the doorman opened the door for her. The driver led her across the impressive lobby, with marble floors, tall pillars, and huge floral arrangements, to an elevator.

"This is a private elevator." He slid a card into a slot and the door opened. "It will take you to the penthouse." Then he handed her the card and walked away.

The door closed and her stomach fluttered as the elevator started moving upward.

When the door opened, she stepped into a huge apartment with windows overlooking the city. She stepped onto the gleaming, dark hardwood floor of the foyer as she stepped from the elevator and glanced around, expecting her benefactor to be waiting for her. But there was no one in sight.

She glanced around at the elegantly furnished penthouse, with light walls and leather couches and chairs. The wood furniture had clean lines and large pieces of abstract art hung on the walls. The whole look was balanced by the softness of the plush carpets and cushions.

She walked across the floor and stared out at the city below. The sun was setting and the windows of the other buildings were bathed in orange light.

"Like the view?" a male voice asked behind her.

A prickle started along the back of her neck, then down her spine.

It wasn't the voice of a stranger.

It was him.

She turned slowly, her heart pounding in her chest.

"Mason?" Astounded, she stared at the man she hadn't seen in eight years.

"Hello, Dana."

The shock at seeing him had sent her totally off balance, but now she remembered the situation.

"Oh my God, you're the one? But… you can't…" she sputtered.

He raised his eyebrow in that way she remembered. “Can’t what? Be the one who takes your virginity?”

Her eyes widened. “That’s right. We just… I mean…”

She stared at him, the man who had left when she was eighteen. The man who’d made her feel special and cared for in a time when she had felt like nothing.

A man who haunted her hottest and most forbidden dreams.

She sucked in a breath of air and tried again. “You’re my stepbrother, for God’s sake.”

About Opal Carew

As a *New York Times* and *USA Today* bestselling author of erotic contemporary romance, Opal Carew writes about passion, love, and taking risks. Her heroines follow their hearts and push past the fear that stops them from realizing their dreams… to the excitement and love of happily-ever-after.

Opal loves crystals, dragons, feathers, cats, pink hair, the occult, Manga artwork, Zentangle, and all that glitters. She earned a degree in Mathematics from the University of Waterloo, and spent 15 years as a software analyst before turning to her passion as a writer. She grew up in Toronto, and now lives in Ottawa with her husband, and three cats. One of her sons just finished a Masters degree at Sussex University in the UK and is now pursuing a second Masters at Carleton University in Ottawa. The other son is working on his undergraduate degree at Carleton University. Yes, mom is proud!

Connect with Opal online:

Newsletter: **OpalCarew.com/newsletter**

Website: **OpalCarew.com**

Facebook: **facebook.com/OpalCarewRomanceAuthor**

Twitter: **@opalcarew**

Pinterest: **pinterest.com/opalcarew/**

Smashwords: **smashwords.com/profile/view/OpalCarew**

Blog: **opalcarewromanceauthor.wordpress.com/**

Email: **OpalCarew@BestRomanceAuthors.com**

###

Manufactured by Amazon.ca
Bolton, ON